# ANFORA

by Don Roth

Order this book online at www.trafford.com
or email orders@trafford.com

Most Trafford titles are also available at major online book retailers.

Printed in Victoria, BC, Canada.

ISBN: 978-1-4269-0979-5

*Our mission is to efficiently provide the world's finest, most comprehensive book publishing
service, enabling every author to experience success. To find out how to publish your
book, your way, and have it available worldwide, visit us online at www.trafford.com*

*Trafford rev. 11/23/09*

www.trafford.com

**North America & international**
toll-free: 1 888 232 4444 (USA & Canada)
phone: 250 383 6864 ♦ fax: 812 355 4082

A journey that is beyond what you where taught in school, two young couples meet an old school friend. They decide to go riding together. What happens.....only one person knows....but he's not telling Who's the stranger and where does he come from? One adventure after another will keep you guessing. Meet Heidi, John, Connie and Tom along with their friends. What they do is all part of the game of survival. Daring schemes that only enhance their chance of escaping. You'll meet many characters, most of them help the young couples. You'll meet "Babe" the computer ... she'll make you laugh now and then, but she's needed in so many ways. If you've never been on a roller coaster, here's your chance to be on one without leaving your house!

# ANFORA
# Table of Contents

Chapter 1    The Trip ............................................ 1

Chapter 2    Missing ............................................ 12

Chapter 3    The Stranger .................................... 25

Chapter 4    ANFORA............................................ 33

Chapter 5    Routine ............................................ 42

Chapter 6    Plan "A" Plan "B" ........................... 50

Chapter 7    Change of Heart ............................. 64

Chapter 8    Burnwell ......................................... 72

Chapter 9    The Big Night................................... 76

Chapter 10   Encounter ....................................... 92

Chapter 11   Out There ....................................... 102

Chapter 12   The Trial.......................................... 118

Chapter 13   Unknown ......................................... 133

Chapter 14   Return to ANFORA............................ 153

Chapter 15   Dejavu............................................. 167

# Chapter 1

## *The Trip*

*Hodges House Mid-June 6:30 a.m.*
*Allentown, Pennsylvania - 1973*

John - Heidi - You about ready yet?

Heidi - Just a few more minutes.

John - Don't forget we promised to get an early start and we'll still have to pick up Tom and Connie.

Heidi - Ready - hope I didn't forget anything.

John - Don't worry - if we did forget anything we can buy it. We'll, I'm glad we packed and loaded most of our things last night. Off we go. We should arrive at Tom's just about 7:00 a.m. Hope they are ready. Want o beat the traffic out of town.

Heidi - Sighs, shakes her head. I don't know honey. All this rushing around and we don't know where we're going - no planning, nothing.

John - It's an adventure, not a planned vacation. We've been all over this. Relax, enjoy.

Beep, Beep!

Heidi - John, don't beep. Go to the door.

John - Okay.

Well, right on time John. Come on in says Connie, turns to the Winnebago and motions to Heidi to come in.

Connie - Tom will be right down. calls upstairs, Tom!
John and Heidi are here.

Tom - Yes, I know. I heard the horn. Be there in a few seconds.

John - Where are your things; I'll load them aboard.

Connie - They're in the living room. Wait, Tom will help you when he comes down.

John - That's all right; I can handle it. While John is carrying out the suitcases, Connie says, these boys of ours going off to nowhere. No plans, no anything...Funny you should say that. I questioned over and over again.

As a matter of fact this morning just before we left.

Good morning Heidi. Where's John?

Good morning Tom says Heidi. He's loading the suitcases in the wagon.

Tom - Connie, you let John carry our luggage out?

Connie - He's very persistent - you ought to know that.

Tom - Well, I'd better go give him a hand. Tom grabs a few bags. Hey, buddy, doing my job?

John - Well if you got your ass out of bed in the morning... laughs. They both laugh.

The girls looking out the window - now what are they laughing at?

Come on, girls, let's get started!

Tom- Now before we leave, do you have everything?

Connie - Stop treating me like a baby.

John - I'll take the wheel and you can take over later.

Tom - You bet!

Heidi - I'd like a chance to drive too.

The guys look at each other - both shake their heads - Nah.

Heidi - Please!

John - I'll think about it.

Tom - Turns to Connie - if John lets Heidi drive you'll want to too.

Connie - No way, count me out!

Let's head west as Greely said. John starts up the RV and they were on the road...heading west. After several states passed by, nothing of interest seemed to satisfy everyone.

They found a trailer camp and stayed the night. The following morning after breakfast they were on the road... heading west.

Heidi - I knew this so called adventure would be a disaster.

John - Easy, honey, we're only one day out. We're bound to find something. Four days out and now John, Tom and Connie were wondering if Heidi was right. But lo and behold a sign along the road...Stratton Ranch - Fun for All! Twelve miles ahead.

Tom - Hey, maybe we've hit paydirt, game? All agree; let's give it a whirl.

Twelve miles passed quickly.

John - Well, let's hope it's what we want.

Connie - Horseback riding, entertainment, rides, barbeque, the works.

Now Stratton was a large town founded back in 1867 by Ira Stratton. The old man scrimped and slaved for many long years. Every penny he had was invested in land and slowly built a small, but thriving, community. By the late 1800s his first son was born and he grew up. Edward Stratton managed to take over from his Dad and added many more features to its growing empire. In 1916 Ed married. Now his son, Edward Stratton, Jr. had inherited the bulk of the estate.

Present Day 1973

Tom - Looks like a great place. Let's find a hotel. All agree. Not far down the road Connie says, Over there.

Tom pulls in and parks. Well Gang! Here at last. Let's register. They all pile out, grabbing their luggage and enter the hotel.

Tom rings bell

Desk Clerk - May I be of assistance?
We'd like a room please.
Clerk - How many in your party?
Tom - My wife and I.
Clerk - How long will you be staying?
Tom - Ummm...He turns to John. John shrugs his shoulder...holding up three fingers.
Tom - Okay, three days then.
Clerk - Cash or credit card?
Tom - Credit card.
Clerk - Runs credit card through machine. Please register.
Turns book around. Tom signs Mr. and Mrs. Thomas Mon'e, Pennsylvania.
Clerk - First, fifth floor or sixth.
Tom - Fifth, I could use the exercise.
Clerk - We do have an elevator.
Tom - So much for exercise...
Clerk - Your key, sir. Room 512. Boy- bags.
John - Three days for us too. Same floor please.
Clerk - I only have 2 on the sixth, 1 on the first floor.
John - Okay, we'll take the one on the first floor.
Clerk - Cash/credit?
John - Credit card. (Machine run)
Clerk - Please sign the register.
Mr. and Mrs. John Hodges, Pennsylvania.
Your room key 12...boy, bags.
Tom - I should have asked that we be on the same floor.
Clerk - I can change it!
John - NO, that's okay. Let it stay as is.
Clerk - We have a fine western dinner in back of the hotel (points). Show your room key to your waiter and receive a 10% discount.
John - Great...you hear that Tom?
Got it - see you around six in the lobby for dinner.

John - Sounds good. We'll be ready. We have over two hours till then.

That evening they all meet and wander over to the dinner.

Heidi - Dinner! It's gigantic - it's more like a New City restaurant.

Connie to Heidi- That was an understatement. It's awesome.

Tom - Well, let's go in. On entering they all stared around the spacious hall. High timbered ceiling, from the rafters hung large wagon wheels to light the hall. An old-fashioned bar with spitoon and all. On the walls were plowshares, pitchforks, yolks, pictures and murals depicting the by-gone years.

Maitre'de - How many in your party? Four came the reply.

Maitre'de snaps finger...hostess comes over. Follow me please. Everyone is still looking around as the hostess escorted them to a table.

Hostess - How's this?

All agree. Fine, thank you.

Hostess - I'll send back a waitress to help you.

Shortly a waitress approaches their table.

Waitress - Good evening, everyone. My name is Gail and I'll be your waitress for this evening. Everyone smiles and says Hi.

Waitress - Your menu and wine/liquor list. Would you care for a drink before dinner?

Tom - Ladies first.

Connie - I'll have a white wine.

Heidi - A Shirley Temple please.

Waitress - Very good. Gentlemen?

Tom - Large beer, Sam adams.

John - Sounds good, make that two.

Waitress - I'll be back soon with your drinks. (Leaves)

After some small chit-chat the waitress brings the drinks -white wine for you, Shirley Temple for you and two beers.

Enjoy your drinks. Just raise your hands if you need me.

Soup and salad bar is to your left.

Tom - Thank you. All looking at their menus.

John - Have you reached a verdict! All laugh...

Tom - Well, again, ladies first.

Heidi - They have lobster here. But way out west? How fresh and good could it be?

John - I'll ask the waitress when she returns. Anyway, pick something else just in case. After everyone decides, Tom raises his hand. The waitress saw and responded.

Tom - Okay, Gail, we're ready to order. Just one thing.

Waitress - Yes sir.

The girls were wondering about the lobster...frozen?

Waitress - No sir. Mr. Stratton insists all seafood, live lobster be flown in every day...guaranteed fresh.

Tom - Well girls?

Both - The lobster.

Waitress - Gentlemen?

Tom - Steak, medium rare, baked potato and corn.

John - I'll have the prime rib, baked potato and string beans.

Waitress signals to the bus boy to clear the salad dishes.

Hope you enjoyed the salad bar. I'll place your order and would you care for more drinks?

John - Yes, all around. Thank you.

Gail leaves and bus boy clears the table. Moments later Gail returns with the drinks. I forgot to ask if you're guests of the hotel. Ten percent discount if you're a guest.

Tom and John show room keys.

Gail - You didn't have to show me your keys. I'd have taken your word. Here's an itinerary; what to do, where to go, what to see.

As they were leaving the dinner Connie says, Look Heidi, over there. If I'm not mistaken it looks like Lucy.

Heidi - You're right. I think it is...excuse us guys. We see our old school friend over there.

John - I see her, yes, that's Lucy Ferguson. The girls rush over. Lucy? Lucy turns around - yes? Oh, my word, Lucy exclaims.

Heidi - Connie - It's been years. How are you two?

Connie - We're great and yourself?

Lucy - Excuse me, this is my husband, Paul, and I feel great.

Heidi - Join us in a drink, but first I would like you to meet our husbands.

Lucy - Let me guess. John Hodges and Tom Mon'e. Both together since high school.

Connie - Your memory is better than mine and you're right - the boys remember you too. They'll be glad to see you again.

Heidi waves to John and Tom to come over.

Tom - Well, it was you. How have you been?

John - Hi, Lucy, long time no see.

Lucy - Boys, this is my husband, Paul Burrows. Chit-chat goes on for a while and John asks...by the way, Paul, what do you do for a living?

Paul - I teach chemistry at college back home.

John - What do you know, an egghead!

Heidi raising her voice an octave or two. John, that's not nice.

Paul - I'm sure John didn't mean anything derogatory...
Besides, Lucy has called me a lot worse.

Lucy - Okay Paul, stop it!

Time passed and the boys started calling Paul, Professor and Paul didn't seem to mind.

Later on after a few drinks together, Connie says we haven't anything scheduled for tomorrow, but whatever it is, are you game?

Of course came the reply.

Heidi - Great, call you later tonight. What's your room number?

Paul - Cabin twenty-four "C".

Tom - Cabins...we didn't know they had cabins too! Paul - Oh, yes...you can rent tepees too. They have many things here. We've been here six days and only have seen a small part.

John - Well, we better be off to see this town...so goodnight Lucy - Prof. See you tomorrow.

Everyone said goodnight and they went their separate ways. Afterward they took a tour of the town taking in the sights. Heidi - Everyone here is in western outfits. I feel out of place.

John - I can fix that...to the clothing store. Tom - I'm with you guys!

Connie - If the guys buy, I'm with you too.

Tom - With all that settled...let's spend!! spend!! spend!! All laugh.

Tom - According to this map a clothing store is two blocks up on the opposite side of the street. Moments later, after crossing the street they enter. As the clerk came over (all talking at once). Please, one at a time. Connie - We'd like to see some western outfits.

Clerk - I presume for all of you.

John - Yes...hats and boots, the whole nine yards.

Clerk points - Help yourselves. If you need assistance, don't hesitate to ask.

After they selected and paid for the outfits, they thanked the clerk.

You're welcome. Come again soon.

Tom - Finished? Let's go home.

John - One more stop. Heidi and I have been going over the itinerary - how about renting some horses and heading out early a.m. Okay, just one more stop, then we can call it a day.

Tom - All right, let's make it fast - I'm getting tired and I guess the girls are too.

John - The stables are close by, it shouldn't take long.

Here we are, says John. Let's get some help. A while later they had rented horses for the following morning.

Heading back to the hotel it started to rain; then the rain became more intense. All four ran in pouring rain and were glad to reach the hotel. Everyone was soaked. They said good night. Each couple was glad to be indoors. Now for a hot shower and bed.

Later that night Heidi calls Lucy. We've reserved two horses for you and Paul, taking for granted you'll go riding with us. Perfect, replies Lucy. When and where? Tomorrow came the reply. Stratton Stable - west side at 7:30 a.m. We'll wait for you.

Lucy - Great, Heidi. See you tomorrow. Good night.

Heidi - Bye.

The following morning six of them struck out for the stables.

Red - (ranch hand) had selected the horses.

Each party had a canteen and some sandwiches and off they went.

Forty-five minutes later:

We're just a short distance now.

John - Hey, my horse is limping. Hold on. John dismounts, checks. He has a stone in his shoe. You go on ahead. I'll catch up with you.

Tom - Okay. We'll tie the horses over by those shrubs and start up the Summit.

Heidi - I'll stay with you, honey.

John - No, it's okay. Go on, I'll catch up.

Heidi - Are you sure?

John - Uh huh. Go.

John takes out a hunting knife, finds the stone and dislodges it. He decided to walk the horse around a while to make sure he was okay. Now you're okay, boy. Let's play catch up.

Meanwhile the other five had moved up the trail. Connie sets up a video camera on a tripod. Tom is busy loading his camera while Heidi explored the surroundings. As Heidi proceeds to look around, over a small rise she spots a flower; a beautiful flower the likes of which she has never seen before! She runs back. Connie, Lucy, come see this. Connie picks up the video camera tripod and all. Tom and Paul rush after. There, says Heidi, pointing to the flower.

Wow, says Connie. I've never seen this species before. What about you, Paul? Paul shakes his head no. Connie sets up tripod and video and turns on the camera. Every-body get around the flower. I think you may have found a new species, says Paul. If so, we can call it the "Heidi Orchid".

Connie - How do you know if it's an orchid...orchids don't grow in this part of the country.

Paul - Can't be sure, but it looks like one.

Tom - I'll take some snapshots.

It no doubt was an orchid. How did it get to be here? It was twice the size of most varieties with delicate colors, white changing to violet at its center, brown and black speckles dotted the surface of the violet. The outside petals were a brownish orange covering the white,and violet interior. Heidi was ecstatic with her find. As they were picture-taking and admiring the huge flower, Heidi looked UP and let out a blood-curdling scream.

Back down the trail (about 100 yards) John was just about to tie up his horse when he heard the scream! Heidi, Heidi, John yells, drops the reins and races up the trail. At the crest he can make out the group, Heidi laying on the ground.

John runs as fast as his legs will carry him. Oh God! Oh God! His heart was racing like a horse on a long stretch of bad roadway. He was getting closer now. Please God, help! Just a matter of a few more yards. Jutting out from under a rock a tree root..,John didn't notice it and he tripped over it at top flight...sommersaulting through the air. Thud!

Tom runs over to John as Connie and Lucy look on in horror, blood everywhere. Meanwhile Paul is trying to revive Heidi. Tom - He has a pulse but is bleeding profusely from his head. He's out cold.

# Chapter 2

## *MISSING!*

Calvi Burnwell was now in his third term as Sheriff ( duly elected ) he had hired Sarah, ( the girl he loved since high school )as secrectary and dispatcher. Cal had seven dupties: Len, Will, Sam, Earl,Rich, chuck Andy. Calvin was called Sheriff by his men, but for most part Cal for short.

Cal - Sarah! I'm going over to the dinner. Call if you need me. ( same line every morning ) and as usual....Cal don't forget your thermos. Oh! thanks Sarah. Cal was also a creature of habit, heading away and across the street to Bill and Coral Cafe. Entering the cafe, good morning Cal. Good morning fellas!.

Cal seats himself at the end of the counter. Good morning Cal. Usual ? Not today says Cal handing her his thermos. Let me talk to your hubby. Sure came the reply. Bill! Cal wants to talk to you!

Bill wiping his hands on his apron.....What's up CAL!??

Cal I would like something different this morning.

As you know for the last three years i've ordered the samething each and every morning! Need a change Bill, need a change!

Check out our menu, Then I'll make extra special, hows that.

Cal I'll leave it up to you.

Bill - -gotcha!

Cafe phone rings.

Cora and Bill's Cafe. yes... yes...yes...okay. bye Cal, sarah just called, you're needed back at your office ASAP Cal, okay, tell Bill to cancel that order. I may be back later.

Cal scurries to the door. Hold on Cal, your thermos.

Cal thanks Cora.He returns, grabs his thermos,looking back Cora call Sarah and tell her I'm on the way!

At the office, What's up Sarah? Sarah - Ed's in your office, wants to see you.

Cal- What about?

Sarah - Don't know, better see him. Cal enters his office,Good morning Ed.

Ed - morning Cal. I may have a problem on my hands.

Cal - Go ahead.

Ed - Well, Red over at the corral had rented some horses out to a group of easterners. One horsecame back.no rider. They went out to the butte.

Cal - Go ahead.

Ed - Red knows more then I do, you'll have to ask him.

Cal - We'll take my squad car over.

Ed - I have my own outside.I'll follow.

Cal - Sarah get one of the boys to meet me at Ed's corral.

Sarah - I'll send whoever is closet.

Cal - Thanks Sarah.

At the corral Ed sees Red. Waves him over.

Ed - Tell Cal about the couples that left yesterday morning.

Red - Good morning Sheriff

Cal - Good morning Red. What 's happening here?

Red - Six people went up to the butte and never came back.....Red is interupted as deputy Len pulls up.

Hey Sheriff - Sarah said to get right over here!

Cal - fine Len. Glad you're here. I'm going over to the butte to look arround. Talk to Red.and get a full description of the party and other information that maybe necessary. Then meet me at the butte.

O.K. says Len.

Cal drives off to the butte.

Len - Now how many in the group?

Red - six.

Len - Give me a full description, height, weight, color of hair, etc etc.

Red - Gives only what he can remember. One thing for sure, they wanted to be back for the Big Shindig.

I told them it would start at 6:00 P.M. there would be dancing and a barbecue, they said they wouldn't miss it!

Red- Three things: (One) No camping equipment; (Two)

One sandwich each and 6 canteens of water; (Three)

The girls wanted to go to the shindig and they said they would be back around 6:00 p.m.

Len - Why didn't you call the Sheriff's office when they didn't show up?

Red - I got off at 4:30 that day and came to work this morning around 7:30 a.m. That's when I discovered one of the horses (rented out) to one of the six that left yesterday morning.

Len - Okay, Red, that's that, thanks.

Len gets in his squad car and heads for the Butte.

Arriving at the Butte, Len parks his car next to the Sheriff's car...he calls out...Sheriff!

Over here Len came the reply.

Len - Got a description and everything like you asked.

Cal - Wasn't sure if we needed it or not. But we do!

Look here, the horses are still tied up. Follow me up the trail and bring along some yellow tape. I'll show you where to cordon off what area.

Okay, Sheriff. I don't want anybody here until we discover what's going on.

I ventured about a hundred to a hundred fifty yards.

That's as far as the prints go.

Len - Then they never went up to the top. It's still over two miles to the top, but the prints end here.

Len - Two miles - they would never make it back by 6:00 that night.

Cal - What do you mean 6:00 p.m.

Len - According to Red they were planning to be back by six for the shindig.

Cal- Wonder why Red never told them they couldn't possibly ride out here and see the top of the Butte in that space of time? Tape this area off. You'll see many tracks leading from here. But one set of prints seem to be walking a horse around. I assume one of the male riders had a problem with his horse, dismounted as the rest went on alone.

Len - Maybe that's the horse that came back.

Cal - Of course, only five here. Let's check here where they stop. Len taping as they walk along, you'll notice after last night's rain, prints are very clear; I count 2 male prints, three female prints walking at a leisurely pace while another set of male prints are long-strided as he must have been running from down there to up here. Hold on!

I didn't see this before!

Len - What is it?

Cal - Appears to be human blood.

Len - Where!

On the rocks there, points, those long strides - tripped and fell - maybe his blood? That explains all the prints around.

Len - Look over there, more prints.

Cal - Seems some came over to aid their fallen comrade, while the others stayed over there? But why...why? Here's what I think happened. One male stayed behind to tend to his horse for a reason. Possible stone in shoe or loose saddle while the rest ventured up here. Some-thing must have happened over here and he came running!

Len - That's good Sheriff...but where are they?

Cal - Your guess at this time is as good as mine! Look Len, finish roping off this area. I'm going back to the office. Use your bullhorn off and on - call out every fifteen minutes or so. Maybe we'll get lucky! I'm going back. If anything turns up buzz the office. I'll be sending over a lab man. Cal arrives at the office.

Sarah - You're back. What did Ed want.

Cal - Seems three couples went to the Butte and were to be back at 6:00 p.m. The following morning one horse came back alone...no rider. Len is up there roping off the area - can't find a soul...did find blood.

Sarah - Human blood?

Cal - Not sure, but would like you to send someone from the lab to check. Len will be waiting for him. Then call all deputies in. We may have to form a search party; that's if Len doesn't spot them. Meanwhile I'll be at the radio station. Then I'm going back to relieve Len.

Cal sees Len. Len, finished?

Len - All done. Met the lab man and he took a sample of the blood. Also, as I was roping off the area I found what appeared to be a new hunting knife. I gave it to the lab guy to check for blood.

Cal - Very good, Len. What, if anything, did you find out about the group.

Len - Not much. Called every fifteen minutes...no response. In between time I got my binoculars out and scanned the area...zero.

Cal - Okay, Len, go back to the office and wait for me.

Len leaves and Cal does a little more investigating.

Both Len and Cal spotted the video and cameras, yet nothing was done about them. On inspection, Cal noticed the video camera was blinking red. It was losing power. This means the camera had been on since yesterday! (Could it tell him something?) Grabbing the video cassette and 2 small cameras he heads back to his car. One more glance around...he leaves.

2:45 p.m. Sheriff's Office

Sarah - Cal, the men will be here by 3:00 p.m. sharp.

Cal - Any word from the lab?

Sarah - Not yet, Cal.

Cal - On your way home tonight would you drop off these rolls of film for developing? Need ASAP.

Sarah - Sure, Cal.

In his office Cal takes the video tape out, installs, rewinds and waits for the tape to stop.

Now to play and see if there's anything on the tape that's worthwhile.

Sarah - Cal, the deputies are here.

Cal - Be right there...he turns the video off. Leaves office.

Cal - Okay, men, we have three couples missing. One person may be hurt. Each one of you will head a search party. The radio station, if you haven't already heard, has asked for volunteers tomorrow. When they arrive let's hope for a good turnout. They will be equally divided among you. Seven groups should be ample.

However the number of volunteers is uncertain at this time. If we need additional help, there's the National Guard. Len has a description of the missing group.

Sarah will make copies for each of you.

Sarah - Don't look now, Cal, but we've got company.

Swarming outside the office, reporters pushing their way in all shouting at once. Local citizens as well as vacationers. All curious (news travels fast).

Cal - Get these people out. The deputies finally manage to clear the inner office.

Cal - ATTENTION, please. Please, quiet down.

Come on, Sheriff. What gives?

Cal - All right, all right, I can only tell you that a group of vacationers, (2) two couples from Pennsylvania and (1) one couple from Illinois are missing.

Shout from the crowd - I heard someone got murdered!

Cal - Three couples are missing, that's all, nothing more, nothing less.

You're holding out -

Cal - I will not speculate on this. When I know more you'll know!! Now break up and go home. But before you go, if anyone is here to volunteer in the search, come inside and Sarah will assign you to a deputy. The rest go on home. A few came in and signed up.

The radio station reported the missing group and asked for volunteers to help. Report to Sheriff Burwell's office. All volunteers should report the following morning. The time of the search will start sharply at 7:00 a.m.

Cal - Sarah, I feel I'm forgetting something?

Sarah - Lab man?

Cal - No.

Sarah - You mentioned the National Guard.

Cal - Yes, that's it! We may need them. A lot of people work so we may not get as many volunteers as we might hope for. It's still early. See if you can reach the Guard and explain our situation. The deputies are standing around waiting for Cal.

Cal - O.K. men, over here to the map. Pointing at the map. We have a lot of ground to cover. Giving each of you a sector to cover is going to be rough. It's a lot of territory to cover. As you know the more volunteers we get the better for each group. As you heard, Sarah is calling the National Guard. This will definitely help.

Also...phone rings...Sheriff's Office...Yes...thank you, Bye.

Cal - The lab called. It is definitely human blood - no blood found on knife.

Cal - Thanks, Sarah. Please let me know when you have reached the Guard.

Well, men, that's about it for now. Tomorrow morning the map will be marked with your sections. Each group will carry a bullhorn, whistles, flares and a walkie-talkie.

Your descriptions of the six will be passed out tomorrow.

Anyone can report earlier than 7:00 a.m. would be well appreciated.

Sarah - Lieutenant Miles on the phone. Cal picks up the extension.

Hello, Sheriff Burnwell here.

Hello, came the reply. Hear you need our services?

Cal - We sure do!

Lieutenant - I spoke to the Commander of the Post... we're all yours.

Cal - Ya Ho! How many men could you spare?

Lieutenant - As many as you need!

Cal - Could it be 200 plus - big country, you know.

Lt. Miles - My commander stated whatever you need, don't hesitate.

Cal - That's great. My men will be heading out on foot due west and with your men deployed I'd say (60) sixty miles out heading east we should find them. If that's okay for me to impose my will!

Miles - I for one don't mind following orders. That's what I get paid for. One thing, Sheriff, how's about I throw in a helicopter?

Cal - At this rate if we can't find them...then no one can!

Miles - We can be there by 5:00 a.m. your time, okay?

Cal- Five a.m. is perfect, thanks, goodbye Lieutenant.

Miles - Goodbye, Sheriff.

Sarah - Did I hear you say 5:00 a.m.?

Cal - So I get up extra early after all, for over 200 men and a copter! Who could squabble about time?

Sarah - Well, it's almost quitting time, mind if I leave a little early?

Cal - You've worked hard today as you do every day - it's only fifteen more minutes anyway. See you tomorrow.

Sarah - Goodnight, Cal...oh, by the way. Did you eat today?

Cal - That's another thing I forgot. Sarah shakes her head, grins at Cal. Goodnight again.

Cal - Goodnight Sarah! Cal closes up. The deputies go home.

Cal heads over to the Cafe. The diner has only three people there.

Evening, Cal, says Cora. This is the first time I've seen you this time of day.

Cal - Evening, Cora. Missed breakfast this morning, forgot lunch and just too busy all day. Sarah reminded me to eat, else I'd be on the way home with an empty stomach.

Cora - Well then you must be starved? What'll you have?

Cal - If the grill is open I'll take something quick, have to be up before 4;00 a.m. tomorrow.

Cora - I've heard the radio, but what's with 4:00 a.m.?

Cal - The National Guard will be here at 5:00 a.m.

Cora fried up two hamburgers, some home fries and got out a cola.

Cora - Hum?

Cal - I wish these people would show up and we could call this whole thing off and get back to normal.

After dinner Cal says his farewell and heads for home. It's been a long day for Cal, and it looks like it will be another one tomorrow. Entering into his apartment he throws his hat, off comes the shirt and tie, hangs up his gun, throws some cold water on his face, sets his alarm clock, grabs a beer and goes into the living room. He turns on the television and sits down in his recliner. While pondering he slowly drifts off.

Buzz...buzz...buzzz came from the alarm from the other room. Rising from the chair...four-twenty already!

One good thing - he was partly dressed - pants and boots still on - he washes, runs into bedroom, shuts off alarm. Donning clean shirt and tie he grabs his hat and gun, leaves the apartment with television still on.

arriving at the station Cal is surprised the door is unlocked and the lights are on.

Sarah - Good morning, Cal.

Cal - What are you doing here so early?

Sarah - In ten minutes Lt. Miles will be here plus the volunteers and the deputies right behind. You'll need some help.

Cal - I'm still not quite awake yet - fell asleep in the chair last night and I didn't have time for a cup of coffee to knock out the cobwebs.

Sarah - Way ahead of you. Made a pot of coffee. It's in your office.

Cal - Whoa! Thanks!

Sarah - Don't let me forget my coffeepot tonight.

Cal - Me? Remind you!

Sarah smiles.

Five a.m. and Lt. Miles is right on time.

Lt. Miles - Good morning. I'm Lt. Miles here to see Sheriff Burnwell.

Sarah - Go right in (points to office). He's expecting you.

Lt. Miles enters office. Sheriff Burnwell?

Yes, yes says Cal. Come right in. They shake hands.

Lt. Miles - My troops are on the outskirts of town waiting instructions.

Cal - Good. I may have some pictures of the missing group.

Lt. Miles - That will help.

Cal - Grab some coffee. I'll show you the map. This is the area I'd like your men to take. By the way, how many men at your disposal?

Lt. Miles - One hundred seventy-two plus one helicopter.

Cal - Great. Now, as I was saying, this area to the west of the Butte (here) have your men spread out from this point to here and head east. My deputies and volunteers will be disbursed along this line at the foot of the Butte and head west.

Lt. Miles - The helicopter can cover all this area plus the Butte.

Cal - Exactly. Now when the photographs arrive I'll send them out. In the meantime all we can do is give you a description.

Lt. Miles - Well, Sheriff, you've got it covered. If there's anyone out there, we'll find them.

Cal - My men will start at seven. This is plenty of time for you to deploy your troups.

Lt. Miles - If we spot them we'll send up a flare.

Same here replies Cal. Also Sarah will give you a description before you leave.

(Lt.Miles proceeds out of town to join his men.)

Cal - How soon will the photos be ready Sarah?

Sarah - Had a rush on them. I told him we needed them before seven o'clock today.

Cal - Now we wait for the boys and volunteers.

Six-thirty rolls around and the photos arrive along with several dozens of volunteers. Deputies, one by one roll in.

Cal - Andy, take these photos out to Lt. Miles. He's located here...then report back ASAP. You'll be heading Group One.

Andy - Yes, Sheriff.

(Andy races out of town.) More volunteers arrive.

Cal - I estimate about one hundred or so volunteers - okay you deputies to the map once more.

(After the map showing and designated position, they are just about ready.)

Sarah - Andy's back!

Cal - Send him in. O.K. Andy, you and your Group 1 are here. Now, men, everyone be sure you have whistles, bull horn, walkie-talkies and flares.

Maintain your distance between groups, but not out of sight. So far we only have a little under two hundred.

But we still have some stragglers showing up. O.K. let's get out to the Butte. All you volunteers follow the deputies out and each one pick a deputy to follow when you get there. If you need me, I'll be back here. All cars and seven deputies leave town.

Sarah - Well, Cal, that wasn't so bad.

Cal - I cut it too short. I should have allowed more time. It takes at least a half hour to get to the Butte from here and they just left.

Sarah - So they're fifteen minutes late arriving.

Cal - I suppose.

Sarah - More people coming!

Cal rushes outside, more volunteers. Everyone listen, head out to the Butte. My men just left.

O.K., Sheriff!

At the foot of the Butte, the Deputies take their assigned positions. So far, each group has just sixteen men or so apiece. Just as they were starting out, the volunteers from town arrived adding another 20 men to each group. Now they would not be so spread out. The signal to start... Lt. Miles had his men spread out and began to arrive east. Precisely at seven a.m. the Sheriff's group, now organized, set out seven-thirty-three. The search was now officially started.

As the day wore on. the army group under Lt. Miles were within fifty yards of Cal's group. It was almost five o'clock when they finally met.

NOTHING.

Well, Lt. Miles - No luck either, says Deputy Len?

Not a soul. It's as if the earth had swallowed them up, replies Lt. Miles.

I'll call the Sheriff says Len. Ring.

Sheriff's Office.

Hi Sarah, Len here. Let me talk to the Sheriff.

Buzz...Line one Cal, it's Len.

Cal - Go ahead Len.

Len - No luck, what now?

Cal - You and the boys come back and send the volunteers home. Put Lt. Miles on.

Len - Lt. Miles, the Sheriff would like to speak to you.
Hello, Sheriff.

Cal - Hello, Lt. I just wanted to thank you and your men for helping us. I guess we can call off the search.

Lt. Miles - While we're here, what about the east end of the Butte?

Cal - High range. They'd have to have climbing gear for that. West was the only way to go. Besides, One man was wounded.

Lt. Miles - Well, then that leaves that out. Sorry we couldn't find them.

Cal - Everyone tried their best. That's all one can do. I told my deputy to come in and disperse the volunteers.

Lt. Miles - Well, Sheriff, it's been nice meeting you.
Cal - Same here.
Lt. Miles - Call us again if you need us. Goodbye Sheriff.
Cal - Thanks, Lt. Bye.
Cal thinks to himself...where are they?

# Chapter 3

## *The Stranger*

Tom was busy reloading his camera. Connie was adjusting the video camera as Lucy and the Professor were right next to Heidi looking at the orchid...when Heidi looked up she saw a tall, helmeted figure just feet away. She screamed, Lucy was to shocked to scream. As Heidi fell forward, Paul caught her. Connie was shaking as Tom came over to her.

The tall stranger looked down and said, don't be frightened...I won't hurt you.

Tom - Who are you?

Before the stranger could say, John appears, trips and is knocked out cold.

Tom rushes over to John and says he has a pulse, but is bleeding profusely from his head. He's out cold. We have to get him to town as quick as possible, says Paul.

Tom - He's bleeding too much and we're too far from town.

Tom turns to Connie...Get me something to wrap around his head.

Meanwhile Heidi comes around, sees the stranger but more importantly she sees Tom leaning over John.

Heidi - John, honey.

Tom - He fell. I'm trying to stop the bleeding now.

The Stranger - I can help. He touches his left arm... seven to beam up.

All arrive aboard the space craft. The guys are spell-bound and the girls huddle together.

John will be well taken care of assures the stranger.

John is put in a disinfection chamber...moments later he is whisked off to the medical facility.

Next the others enter the chamber. Moments later the stranger enters. As he emerges all eyes focus on him. Not only was he tall (six feet five) but he had a large cranium, brown hair, brown eyes. Other than his larger head, he looked human. The girls were frightened, but Heidi spoke up first... where's my husband?

Stranger - He's being attended to in our infirmary.

Heidi - May I see him?

Stranger - As soon as I get word.

Tom - Who are you?

Stranger - Lieutenant Sibira, you may call me Sibi.

Tom - Well, Sibi - How did we get here and where are you from.

Sibi - I'm from the Planet Anfora and you were beamed aboard our space craft.

Tom - It all happened so fast, first we were talking about John and the next thing we were going through a chamber of some sort. Then you came out and I knew you weren't human...So we were beamed up! Sounds like science fiction.

Sibi laughs. If I were in your place I wouldn't believe it either. Sorry to scare you twice in one day. Your friend needed medical attention right away so I beamed us aboard.

Prof - Sibi, when we first saw you, you were wearing as I would describe it, a space suit, metallic green in color, large helmet, with two large bug like eyes, an apparatus on both sides of the helmet that extended to your backpack which I assumed was your breathing source.

Sibi - Very observant the re...

Prof - Sorry, but I wasn't finished. I realize now it was oxygen for we are all breathing the same air. I would also wear a spacesuit for space travel, but the goggles are so large?

Sibi - Not always knowing what we may encounter. The designers came up with twelve (12) different lenses for each eye. Each eye contains six lower lenses and six upper lenses to be used singularly or in any combination.

(Over speaker in Anforian language.)

Lt. Sibira, report to Commander Zoc's quarters.

Sibi - That call was for me. I have to go, be back later to assign you some quarters. In the meantime, I'll have one of the crew show you to our food galley. Bye.

All - Bye, Sibi.

At Zoc's Quarters...

Sibi - Of course, Sir. I'm to blame for the injury of one of them. He's badly hurt. He may have died if I didn't bring him aboard.

Zoc - I see...the lowest ranking member of our crew know to scan the surrounding area before they leave... Did you?

Sibi - No, Sir!

Zoc - Why not?

Sibi - This being my first voyage and my first patrol, was anxious to complete my mission.

Zoc - You forgot. I'll let it pass this time...but in the future, think before you act. Dismissed.

Sibi - Thank you, Sir! Salutes.

(Sibi returns to the five.)

Tom - Everything all right?

Sibi - Fine. Commander Zoc is very understanding.

Heidi - Can I see my husband?

Sibi - I'll check in right now. Sibi calls ahead... O.K., fine. Hangs up. You can see him now says Sibi.

He's still asleep, but he's fine. I'll take you to him. The others may come too. Only one visitor at a time is allowed. At the infirmary Sibi leaves Heidi with Nurse Ada. Follow me says Ada. He's right over here. Looks as if he's coming around!

Heidi - Honey, it's me, Heidi.

John opens his eyes (things are a little blurry)

John - Heidi - Heidi, are you all right? Slight moan.

Heidi - I'm fine. It's you who got hurt.

John - I heard you scream, I was running...that's all I remember.

Heidi - I'll explain later. Heidi bends over and kisses John. I'm going to tell the gang you're awake, be right back.

Heidi - John's okay. He's awake. She rushes back to John's side.

One by one they visit John, but only for a few minutes.

Nurse Ada made sure of that.

Next morning John is sitting up and looking around (thinks a very unusual room), shrugs.

Nurse Ada comes in.

Morning John, I'm Nurse Ada.

Morning Ada (John squints). Breakfast for you and a visitor too. Ada leaves showing Tom in. Five minutes only now.

Tom - Gotcha!

Tom - How are you feeling this morning?

John - Just a slight headache but my vision goes in and out.

Tom - Blurry?

John - Blurry yesterday but today... Tom - Go on.

John - Some things just don't look right. Tom - How do I look to you?

John - You look normal but this room, Nurse Ada... strange.

Tom - Oh, I see...let me fill you in before my five minutes are up; meantime eat while I talk...and there you are.

John - I must be dreaming.

Tom - No, it's true. Heidi will fill you in on any questions you still have. Oops, here comes Ada... Tom, you must admit one thing though. John - What's that buddy?

Tom - Well, except for the high forehead Ada's pretty good-looking, hey? Bye John.

Ada -I see your friend just left, but you haven't touched much of your meal.

Sorry, Nurse, says John, but I've got a slight head-ache.

Ada reaches into her pocket, brings forth a device. John - A tuning fork?

Ada laughs - no, an electronic device. Place it on the bridge of your nose, prongs on either side. It sends a pulse to relieve pressure and discomfort.

John tries it. How long before it takes effect?

Ada - Only a minute or two; looking at her watch.

How do you feel?

John - It's gone completely.

Ada - I'll leave it here, use it whenever you need to.

It will charge up six to seven times before you have to discard it.

John - How do I charge it?

Ada - Just plug in here for three minutes. Light will turn orange when charged; if no color appears, throw it out.

John is discharged the following afternoon and joins his fellow travelers. Heidi is so pleased to see John up and about, she begins to cry.

Connie - Isn't that romantic, Tom?

Tom - Let's go back to our quarters before I cry.

Prof. - Coming Lucy?

Heidi wipes her eyes; let's go to our quarters too!

John - Are they nice?

Heidi - A-one, plus you can see out the portals.

Soon after came a chiming at their door.

John answers door. Well, hello. You must be Sibi?

You have it - I'm here to inform you and your wife that you and the others have been invited to Commander Zoc's quarters. Heidi and John leave with Sibi. Out in the hall waiting is the rest of the gang. O.K. says Sibi, follow me. The elevator takes them up six decks, stops, they exit. Sibi leads them to Zoc's quarters. Chimes!!! Enter came the answer. Lt. Sibi - They're here sir.

Zoc - Show them in. You may leave Lt. Call you later. Well, good afternoon new friends. I'm Commander Zoc and your names are?

Professor Paul Burrows and my spouse Lucy and these here are Thomas Mon'e and his wife Connie and John Hodges and his spouse Heidi.

Zoc - Glad to finally welcome you. Now John, you are the one who was hurt, am I correct?

John - Yes, Commander.

Zoc - Please not Commander, just call me Zoc. It's easier, yes?

John - Fine with us Zoc.

O.K., now you were brought aboard eleven forty-five your time. Sthree twenty-eight, eight thousand four-hundred sixty-three.

Tom - What's that?

Zoc - A record for my log!

Tom - I still don't get it; all those numbers.

Zoc - Oh, yes. Sthree twenty-eight - that means S for Summer, the last part is the date.

Prof - Three twenty-eight! That's a long month.

Zoc laughs. No. We have no months. Just four seasons; shows them the calendar on the wall. Winter starts our season followed by Spring, Summer and Fall. Just like your seasons. The difference being Winter Day starts number one through the end of the year. It is a continuous number that the last day of Fall would be four hundred fifteen days (415) then back to number one again.

Prof. - Got it. Your days must be longer than ours.

Zoc - Basically the same.

Zoc - Our planet is large but rotates faster. A little longer in a year but twenty-four per day. Tom - We were beamed aboard, but we never saw your ship in space.

Zoc - You couldn't. We're what you call invisible. Radar cannot detect us. And the human eye even with telescope will not see us.

Tom - How is that possible?

Zoc - Asking for classified information?

Tom - No just curious.

Zoc - I'll tell you this much. The exterior absorbs and reflects. Also our ships are completely round.

Tom - I noticed windows or portals, whatever you call them, an over the place. Certainly light will be emitted to the exterior.

Zoc - No. No light can escape. We can see out, no one can see in.

John - You speak English better than some people back home.

Zoc - We'ye been picking up your world languages for the past three thousand years.

John - For what purpose?

Zoc - Some day in the future when your Earth evolves to a peaceful unity, our world will contact yours. Up to now your planet is still in conflict with his neighbor, therefore until there's peace on your planet, our people will not be in contact. Any questions?

Heidi - When do we go home?

Zoc - It may be a while.

Heidi - Why?

Zoc - My ship is on a mission to collect rare species of plants for medical purposes. We've been in search for some time and located such a plant on Earth. Lt. Sibira was sent down. He had been successful in his quest when he happened upon your group.

Heidi - That doesn't answer my question.

Zoc - We've been away a long time. We're heading home.
You will be taken back after our mission is complete.

There was nothing to do but wait it out. They made good their stay on ship, making many new friends among the crew. Those who didn't speak English had other crewmen interpret for them. The language problem wasn't so bad. Weeks turned to months and soon many months passed, feeling as part of the crew and learning more and more about Commander Zoc and the ship itself. John and Tom were most interested in how the ship navigated through space, what type of propulsion used, etc. John was sure he could pilot the craft himself. The ship was programmed by computer. But without the language it would be impossible.

The Professor had asked Sibi if someone could teach them the language. Sibi explained the crew as well as himself hadn't the time to teach, also no language dictionary was aboard. Lt. Sibi told his findings to Zoc.

Zoc tells Sibi the earthlings are very inquisitive about so many things. I wonder.

Sibi - Wonder what Commander?

Zoc - Only my suspicions, nothing more.

Sibi - You think they will take over our ship?

Zoc - Come, come, Lt. That would be quite impossible and you know it.

Sibi - You're right, Sir.

Zoc - Just keep reporting to me. Dismissed.

Sibi salutes and leaves.

More months fly by.

Lt. Sibi calls the earthlings together. I have good news!
(All are in attendance of his words.)

Lt. Sibi - In just three weeks we will have reached Anfora.

# Chapter 4

## *Anfora*

The group, although apprehensive, still looked forward to seeing this new world.

Sibi took them to the observation deck where they peered out into the darkness. Straight ahead loomed Anfora. Still quite a distance away, but still they could make out cloud cover, greens and blues. Sibi says we're still far away but in a couple of days you'll be able to see a lot more.

Prof. - When will we land?

Sibi - My guess, sometime tomorrow afternoon.

Lucy - What season will we be encountering when we land.

Sibi - One hundred- fourteen. That's just two weeks into the Spring season. Leaving the observation deck and heading back to their quarters John says hope the local natives treat us as well as Commander Zoc and the crew has.

Tom - We'll know by tomorrow for sure.

Connie - I'm still worried.

Tom - Calm yourself. We can't do a thing but disembark.

Connie - Just stay close to me.

Prof. - I believe we're facing a friend, not an enemy.

Lucy - I'm with Connie. I'm still worried too!

Heidi - I know we will be treated just fine. After all they did help John and fed and clothed us.

John - I go along with that - not to worry...

Next day

Sibi escorts them to the observation deck once more.

Here we are...looks like we're only one hour to landing time. Take a look now.

It was enormous. More features appeared, great oceans, large land masses. Some areas were still overcast, but all in all a magnificent view.

Sibi - O.K. Lets go down and prepare for landing.

As they buckle themselves in John asks Sibi - Sibi, if this craft is round, how does it land?

Sibi - Wings, how else.

John - You must have hidden them (looking out the portal).

Sibi - Wing, tail, rudder wheels and all will descend outward and downward once we reach the proper altitude.

Brace yourselves, we're about to land. It only seemed like a few minutes passed as the great ship came to a halt. Easy. Yes!, says Sibi. All smile.

Tom - What now Sibi?

We wait for Commander Zoc. He will be escorting you.

Here he comes now. Sibi salutes. Return salute by Zoc.

Zoc - O.K. Lt. Sibi. I'll take over from here. Before you go deliver this to the institute and wait. Then call me. Sibi leaves.

Well, says Zoc. Are you ready to explore my world?

All talking at once - Sure! You bet! Lead on,etc.

Then follow me. I have a car waiting, a short tour, then to your quarters.

Heidi - The air outside is so clean and fresh.

You'll marvel at the way we do and present everything.

Good clean air and the purest of water are just a drop in the bucket, replies Zoc.

Leaving the air field heading for the apartment complex, Zoc points out historic landmarks. He was interrupted when the car phone rang...Zoc here. Yes, done already!

Yes...Hum I'm two blocks away from my apartment. Yes, meet me there. Hangs up. Well, friends, this is your home. I'll show you your apartments (on the fifth floor). Zoc opens door - Your apartments are joined together by those double doors. All apartments have the same layout so I'll just show you one apartment.

Just as Zoc is showing them the rooms Sibi enters.

Sibi - Commander, I'm back.

Zoc - Good - Well friends, I'll be leaving you in good hands. Goodnight.

Goodnight Zoc and thank you. Goodnight Commander, says Sibi. Zoc leaves.

Sibi - Well, I have some money vouchers from the institute (bank) for each of you (hands them out).

Tomorrow I'll show you around our city and you can purchase what you need.

Connie - These vouchers are worth how much?

Sibi - In your money, about six hundred dollars for each couple.

Heidi - Wow! Things must be expensive here.

Sibi - Not in the least. Prices are low and Zoc figures between shopping and food, transport, etc. this should be ample. You'll still have money left over. Zoc has made arrangements from the institute to give you the same amount every other week.

How does your government afford to clothe and feed us every week?

Sibi - It's not our government. It's from Commander Zoc.

Lucy - He must be rich.

Sibi - That he is.

John - How can we ever thank him.

Sibi - He's single, has no one...just assets.

John - Plus he's paying for this apartment?

Sibi - No - he owns the building plus several others.

Prof. - Space travel really pays well!

Sibi - No, it doesn't! Let me explain - (One) you have to have a good education, speak at least one language of another planet. Plus excellent health. (Two) The downside you receive minimum wage. That's the lowest wage possible, (Three) You're away from your home for many years. Being away from home discourages many a would be cadet.

Prof. - Hold on...if he only gets minimum wage, how did he get rich?

Sibi - Everything you want or need is aboard the craft.

No money is needed aboard nor can you collect a salary while on a mission. So all money (wages) are put in the institute while interest compiles week after week, month after month, etc. You get the picture. After a three year tour we'll say, you have a tidy nest egg. I should mention salaries are not based on an eight hour day, but a full day. Don't forget he's a commander too.

His salary has gone up with time and he's been in space exploration programs for more than twenty years.

Tom - If the city is like Zoc, we're in for a lot more surprises.

Sibi - Don't tell Commander Zoc I told you. He's a very private man.

You have our word.

Tom - I'm hungry, could you show us where to dine, Sibi?

Sibi - Zoc never showed you your kitchens! Sibi shows them a wall dispenser with small windows showing pictures of what was available from the apartment galley. Pick up this mike and tell them what picture (food) you wish.

Tom - The dispenser knows English too.

Sibi - Yes, it was programmed for you before you arrived. Also pictures can be deceiving and it is hard to tell what to eat, therefore I suggest you order one (one) of each and you can all sample each dish and decide what you like!

John - Any suggestions, Sibi?

Sibi - What I like you may hate.

John - O.K. then we'll order. Are you going to stay? Sure, why not replies Sibi. When the food arrives it was set on the main table surrounded by the seven. Each one took a small portion to taste and asked questions as to what it was. Sibi explained each entree to the group. All agreed it was excellent. Later the waiter came back to take away the dishes and Sibi said goodnight.

The following morning Zoc was summoned to space head-quarters. Zoc faced charges for bringing the aliens back to Anfora.

Well, Commander Zoc. Are you with counsel?

No sir, came the reply.

Committee Chairman - Very well then Commander. Do you understand the charges?

I do, replies Zoc.

Chairman - What is your defense?

Humanity, Sir!, says Zoc.

Chairman - Humanity!! What's that have to do with these charges?

Beaming down to Earth I inadvertently caused one of them severe injuries. I had no choice but to bring him aboard.

Chairman - Question #1 - Why did you beam down? Why not one of the crew. Question #2 - The others were not hurt, why bring them all aboard?

Zoc - The only one capable of going down was ill at the time. It was essential that the plant we needed had to be obtained. So I went myself. Two - The others were witnesses to what had transpired.

Chairman - That was very commendable of you to take a subordinate's place. But you could have left the others behind.

Zoc - If I had left the others behind with one missing member of the crew, think of what might have happened?

Chairman to Zoc - Please wait in the other room while we discuss your verdict. Zoc salutes and waits in the room.

(Twenty Minutes)

You can go in now, Commander. As he enters the room he thinks to himself, well, there goes my career.

Commander Zoc, the panel has reached its verdict

(Zoc to himself, here it comes).

After deliberating we have come to the conclusion that your beaming down doesn't sound responsible. (First)

You're a full Commander and know only too well a Captain/Commander or any person in charge will never leave the bridge. (Second) You would never encounter anyone (since you would scan the area). We have all come to the same conclusion, that you must be covering up for someone on your staff. We also concluded that a man who has commanded so many missions and without mishap and I may add served for more than twenty years faithfully and risen in rank - a Commander whose men have always come first...therefore, the charges are dismissed!

Zoc salutes! Thank you, Sir.

Chairman - Commander Zoc, before you go, one more thing.

And this is that you are fully responsible for these earthlings.

Zoc - Yes, Sir.

Chairman - Tell your subordinate he's a very lucky man.

Zoc was pleased the way it turned out. Now there were many things to do before his next flight and that could be one week or eight months. He had to find out.

The following day Sibi was scheduled to pick up the earthlings and show them the Great City. But first he has to ask Zoc about the committee hearing and when he would be summoned. (Sibi thought to himself... I dread a committee hearing...what happens to me if I get kicked out of the space program??)

Lt. Sibi finally gets to Zoc's apartment...knock... knock. Come in came the reply.

Ah! Lt. Sibi, how is the group?

Excuse me, Sir...But I'm worrying when the committee will call me!

Zoc - It's all over. You don't have to appear.

Sibi - I don't understand. Did I lose my commission? Am I fired - fined?

Zoc - None of the above. You're a Lieutenant still assigned to me.

Sibi - I can't believe it!

Zoc - Let it go Lt. That's an order. Just drop it.

Sibi - You told them I wasn't responsible - you took the blame?

Zoc - You have to obey my orders period. I said drop it and I mean drop! That's if you still want to be in my command.

Sibi - Yes, Sir...and thanks.

Zoc - Don't you have a tour going today?

Sibi - I'm on my way now, Sir. Salutes - Salute returned.

As Sibi is leaving he turns around/..when's our next flight?

Zoc - I'll be over at dispatch this afternoon. You'll know by tomorrow at the latest.

Sibi leaves and heads for the apartments. On arrival he stops in the lobby and buzzes the Professor's room.

Prof. - Hello

Sibi - Here, Prof., can you tell the others to meet me in the lobby.

Prof. - O.K. Sibi - Will do. Be down in a few minutes.

Piling everyone in the car, Sibi heads for the City.

John - Hey Sibi, what's this car run on?

Sibi - Gas.

John - You use gasoline too?

Sibi - No, natural gas.

Tom - All your cars run on natural gas.

No, replies Sibi. Just some, others are electric/ magnetic and solar. Mostly electric.

Prof. - Must be some battery!

Sibi - No batteries, just electric.

Prof. - ??

Sibi - I'll explain later. Look ahead, there's the City. Before going in they took a moment to look.

It was a blend of old and new. The older seemed to enhance the beauty of the newer buildings. Most were skyscrapers and the smallest of these was one hundred twenty stories. The others loomed much higher. Streets were very broad and had brightly designed tiles throughout the Great City Plaza. Connected to each building were rails running from building to building reaching out four feet and fifty feet off the ground. Small cable cars were suspended from the rails above. There were no cars or transportation to be seen anywhere except for the cable cars.

Sibi - Well, what do you think. Shall we park and go in? Yes!

Sibi - The building here is where we park. Look inside. Parking the car in front of one of the doors while the others peeked inside through the windows. They saw huge ferris wheels (not round, but more "U" shaped). Cars were stored one a top of the other. The door rose (two arms slid under Sibi's car), lifted it only several inches off the ground, brought it in, turned 90° degrees and placed it on the rack...the arms retraced their steps to await the next car. Door closes. After leaving the car, they proceeded to the under-ground tube.

Sibi - Now that we have parked the car we can take the underground tube to our final destination.

John - How long a ride?

Sibi - Only a few minutes. If we were going to the end of the line, it would take one hour.

The group walked down the steps and waited for the tube.

Tom - Is this electric or gas transport?

Sibi - Compressed air! Here comes one tube now.

Connie - It looks like a transparent bullet.

Sibi - The cable cars are also made of the same material.

So climb in and buckle up. Once I close this gull wing door and secure...you'll see. Swoosh....

Tom - What the hell was that?

Sibi - Some ride hey!

John - I think my heart is glued to my backbone!

Sibi - I didn't want to scare you so I didn't tell you how fast this thing goes.

The girls were just sitting there staring.

Sibi - O.K. ladies, snap out of it! Laughs.

Heidi - I'm sure we're okay. It's like a roller coaster.

I'd like another ride.

Sibi - On our return trip. Now that we're here walk around, ride, eat?

Lucy - Let's walk awhile, take in the stores and then eat, okay?

The other girls agree, the guys shrug, why not. So off they went.

After a long day they headed back to the apartment. They thanked Sibi.

Sibi - Went over to Zoc's place.

The group all assembled in one apartment to discuss the day.

# Chapter 5

## *The Routine*

John - I really enjoyed today; more than I expected.

Tom - Those see-through cable cars; some sight just over fifty feet off the ground.

John - Yeah, that was awesome. Heidi and Connie missed out.

Heidi - No way was I going up there in a see-through bottom.

John - Honey, you should have gone - you'd get used to it.

Heidi - Maybe, but I don't think so.

Tom - Trust us, you and my wife. Once you try it you won't want to get off!

John - Besides you did enjoy the tube ride twice!

They're transparent. Heidi - That's different; it was at ground level.

John laughs. Fifty feet off the ground you panic and yet you were thousands of miles above Earth.

Heidi - Yes, but I couldn't see through the bottom of the space ship!

All laugh.

O.K., you win honey...just this one time.

Lucy - What about the stores and restaurants?

Prof. - The food was very good, but none of you including myself bought anything.

Connie - I, for one, was just browsing.

Lucy - Of course we will go back now that we know where to find things. I noticed you guys didn't buy anything either.

John - Can't answer for Tom or the Prof, but I didn't see anything I needed.

Heidi - You need clothes!

Of course I do. But as Connie said, we'll all go back again. Tomorrow's another day.

Prof. - By the way, when are we going back?

Looking around John says whenever. They had talked for hours. It was now time to call it a day.

Meanwhile Lt. Sibi had stopped by Zoc's apartment.

Buzz...Buzz...

Evening Commander Zoc.

Evening came the reply. Lt. Sibi salutes.

Zoc says when aboard my ship, salute me. While we're in civies let's dispense with the saluting. Okay?

All right, Sir. Salutes, oops! Forgot, sorry Sir.

Zoc grins from ear to ear. What am I going to do with you Sibi?

Sibi shrugs. I stopped over to see about our next trip; any word?

Yes, replies Zoc. On or about the three hundred twenty-third day.

Sibi - Great, spring and summer off. Where are we headed this time?

Zoc - I never ask where, just when. Sibi - It would be nice to know.

Zoc - Let it be a surprise...now how did the guided tour go today?

Excellent, we toured a small section of the City and of what they saw they were very impressed. Well, that's that? Impressive?

Sibi - Awe struck is more like it. Is there anything else you would like to know?

Not off hand, Sibi. You can go. Keep me posted. Goodnight.

Sibi - Goodnight, Sir.

Weeks passed and each day was a new adventure. The girls loved the City, but Lucy loved it best. Heidi and Connie were getting homesick. Both of them complained they wanted to go home.

Heidi - When are we going home she says to John?

John - I'll check with Zoc this week. It was the same story Connie expressed to Tom. Just over a week passed when John and Tom approached Commander Zoc.

Zoc, our wives would like to know when do you expect to return us home?

Zoc - In good time my friends, in good time. And when is that, says Tom.

Zoc - I have to wait for an assignment, not before.

John - And when will that be?

Zoc - The space council decides if and when I go.

Tom - It looks like we're stuck till then.

Zoc - Don't you like it here?

John - With all due respect Commander, we do. But the girls, like ourselves, miss our planet.

Zoc - In essence you're homesick!

John - Yes. Can you ask your council?

Zoc - I'll let you know soon. They both thanked Zoc and returned to the apartment.

Well, says the girls. What did he say?

Tom - He's not sure yet.

John - If you ask me, it's a stall.

Heidi begins to cry; we'll never go home!

John - Puts his arms around Heidi. Easy now. Tom and I will find a way.

Tom - Sure we will! For now why don't you both go out and buy some clothes.

That's not going to help, says Connie...tearing.

John - Let's talk to Sibi. He tells us everything. If it's a stall and we're not going home old Sibi will tell us.

Tom - I agree. Sibi is coming over today for another tour. We'll ask him.

John - But just don't blurt it out. Let's be subtle, I think, he'll tell us more.

Tom - Girls, now chin up. Don't let Sibi know you've been crying.

The girls stopped crying and freshened up. The door buzzer summoned. That must be Sibi now.

That's my buzzer. I'll go over. Come Connie (grabs her hand).

Tom answers the door. Welcome, Sibi. Come in. Sibi nods. Wait here. I'll get the rest of the gang.

Knocks on the double door. John opens. Good morning, Tom - good morning.

John - Sibi's here (Tom winks). Oh good, I'll fetch the Professor.

Now that we're all here a little different agenda today, replies Sibi. Going to take you out of the City into what you call the suburbs. This I know you'll love.

John - Lead the way.

After leaving the city behind and enjoying the scenery, Sibi explains the road and signs first.

As you'll notice if you descided to go to this town a yellow sign depicting the town's name and a yellow stripe on the road takes you to your destination. Blue sign, blue stripe another town. Orange sign, orange stripe, etc.

Tom - That's all well and good if you're not color blind.

Everyone laughs including Sibi.

John - All along the route every so many feet apart I've noticed what appears to be round spinning air vents of some sort! What's that for?

Those are not air vents but generators producing electrical current by cars passing by.

Prof. - That's very clever.

Sibi - Efficient too!

Heidi - What's the speed limit?

Sibi - There's no speed limit. All cars are governed by magnetic waves to keep you under a programmed speed and also maintains distances between other cars.

Tom - What happens if a car slows down or stops?

Sibi - All roads are monitored. If such a thing happens all traffic is diverted automatically. A highway vehicle is sent out to assist or remove said vehicle.

John - Diverted automatically?

Yes, to avoid mishaps. It radios to your on board computer, takes over and guides your vehicle around the disabled car. Then it returns control back to you.

Prof. - You could fall asleep behind the wheel and still be safe?

Sibi - Basically you're right. The on board computer does the driving. O.K., let's get off here and visit this small town. If you see anything that strikes your fancy or have any questions, fire away.

Connie - There's not a stop sign or traffic light in sight.

Sibi stops the car and points. You'll notice all streets have overpasses and underpasses throughout the towns.

There are no intersections at all.

John - Say we get off at the wrong intersection by mistake?

Sibi - Simple. Look over there, a cross with a "tee" in the center. You get off the highway, street or road, you take the wrong exit, you just follow it halfway around, enter onto the road again and proceed. A full circle will bring you back to where you came from. It's quite an engineering marvel. As the "tee" part of the highway goes under and over, the circle which encompasses the four corners of the "tee" rises at these points, then lowers after each section and raises at each end; sort of a roller coaster ride raising to the different sectors.

Prof. - It looks like a giant knot.

Sibi - Probably. It's hard to describe.

John - you described it fine.

Thank you, says Sibi. Now we need some gas.

Tom - There's a station pointing ahead. They stop to get gas. The station looked similar to a double quanset hut, four entrances, one entrance to a small gift shop, another a clothing store, the other a diner on our side of the station. In the center of the building joining all four sections were the toilets and washroom. Once you were ready to leave you could visit any shop from here without going all around the building. After gassing up, they parked and went into the diner.

It was getting late now and time to head back.

John - Do you have anything planned for us tomorrow?

Not really, why?

John - I was thinking about the space center. How about going there?

Sibi - Didn't Commander Zoc show you it already?

John - Yes. Just a glimpse at a distance, that's all.

Sibi - O.K. space center tomorrow. Tom looks at John and frowns??

Sibi drops them off. See you tomorrow then. After leaving them off Sibi heads home. In the hallway Tom takes John aside. Okay says Tom What's on your evil mind?

John - Prof., join us downstairs.

Prof. - What's up?

John - I'll tell you both outside.

Heidi - What's all the whispering about?

John - I'll fill; you in later honey. It's boys night out.

Lucy - Boys night out!

Prof. - I guess John wants to do or say something. Be a good girl, go on in.

Connie - Well, let's go in girls. We know when we're not wanted.

Tom shakes his head.

The girls retire.

Okay, John, what's up?

John - Not here, outside of prying eyes. Now that we're alone I can tell you, and by the way only tell your wives in private and out of sight of other people.

Tom - Of course!

Prof, nods in agreement.

Okay, says John as you know our wives are homesick. Zoc has given us the run around. I know you feel the same way as I do about this world; it's beauty, culture, the City, everything. It's engineering and so on.

Tom - Get to the point, Buddy. I'm getting to it. I may have a plan, it all depends on our trip out to the space center.

Tom - You're not suggesting...

John - No, not yet, but a possible solution.

Prof. - And what would that include?

John - Your full understanding and cooperation.

Tom - Naturally i'm always with you come hell or high water!

John - Tomorrow mentally note all segments of the space center's security, layout of the building and access to the electric power sources.

Tom - This sounds juicy, go on.

John - Each one of us will have to do our share, agreed?

Tom - Natch...but Prof, you haven't said a word.

Prof. - I'll help of course if the thing you're planning makes sense.

Tom - I know the girls will help.

John - Of that I'm positive.

Tom - Then tonight we can tell our wives.

John - No, not yet. Let's not get them involved until after the space center and a few more things we must do first. No reason to get their hopes up.

Tom - You're right. What are the other things you mentioned?

John - Our apartment computer. When I get back to the apartment I want you there Tom and you Prof. I'll need your chemistry knowledge before the end of this week.

Prof. - Do you want me at the apartment tonight?

John - No, just Tom. He's the computer designer. That's it for tonight.

Tom - We should all agree on telling our wives some story. You know they'll be asking. Any suggestions?

Prof. - We've been gone less than a half hour. What could we tell them for such a short span of time?

Tom - Just tell them it's a surprise?

John - It might work! Anyway, about tonight, I forgot Heidi's home so I'll talk about the computor tomorrow when we get back.

Back so soon, says Heidi? That didn't take long.

John - Not long at all. I just remembered, we never got to ask Sibi about our going home.

John - With so much going on today I plumb forgot.

# Chapter 6

## *Plan A - Plan B*

The next morning Sibi returns to take the group out to the Space Center.

Good morning one and all says Sibi. Good morning came the reply.

John - Sibi, do you know when the next flight out for you and Zoc is?

Sibi - Six weeks from now I'm told.

John - Earthbound?

Sibi - Only Zoc knows. Tom whispers some subtlety to John.

John - Shh - so it wasn't subtle.

Tom - And we still don't know.

Sibi - Anything wrong, gentlemen?

Tom - Nothing Sibi, just a little small talk. Well now that we're here, what would you like to see first?

John - May we see the working of the Space Center and how it operates, the control room, flight deck, all of it, if possible.

Sibi - I don't see why not.

There were many buildings in the area. Tom asked, before we go into the building, I'd like to know what those other buildings were. Sibi points to each building. That one is the hangar where the crafts are overhauled and repaired, if necessary. Those over there are parts offices and the last one is the Power Station.

Tom - Only one power station?

Sibi - Yes! It's quite adequate.

John - Those last two buildings?

Sibi - #1 Storage and #2 Storage.

John - After our tour of the Control Tower, would it be possible to see the Power Station?

Sibi - There's nothing there, just generators.

John - I just want to compare it with what our world has.

Sibi - I'm sure they're similar.

John - Come on, Sibi.

Sibi - All right, if you insist.

John - Thanks, Sibi.

Entering the ground floor of the Control Tower Tom asks, where's your men's room.

Down the hall on your left. Tom nudges John, motions with his head. John gets the message. Excuse us, be right back. Inside the bathroom Tom says what the hell are you doing...you're too obvious.

John - You're right, I'll slow down. Otherwise Sibi will get suspicious.

Tom - I'm glad it finally dawned on you. It's not like you, now relax, buddy.

John - Subtle...subtle...o.k. let's get back.

They spent most of the morning at the Control Tower and part of it at the Power Station (you could see the girls were bored out of their minds). The last thing was to see several of the space crafts. Many subtle questions about its operation, fuel consumption, computers, etc. After a full day they returned home.

Sibi left and went straight to Zoc's home. Meanwhile back at the apartment the girls let loose. It was sure a dull tour. Why did you drag us along? We could have done something else. This went on for a while.

Sorry girls, tomorrow you three can do whatever you wish.

Connie - I wonder if we could rent a car. Tom - It's worth a try. The cars practically drive themselves.

Prof. - I'm sure Sibi will let you drive his car! The boys and I could go on our own too.

Lucy - You mean we separate?

Prof. - Why not?

Heidi - I always feel safe among you guys.

John - Sibi will be with you.

Heidi - Even so. Every where we go people stare at us.

John - That's to be expected. We're a rarity around here.

Heidi - You're right, honey, we'd stare at them too if they were on our world.

Sibi arrives that evening and reports to Zoc. Well, Sibi, what do you have to report? It's strange, but today we went to the Space Center.

Zoc - I wonder why they wanted to go there again? For one thing, they sure were interested in the complex as a whole (one) the Control Tower, (two) the space crafts themselves (third) and most curious about the Power Plant.

Zoc - The Power Plant! Hmm! Something afoot, I'm sure.

Sibi - They were most curious about our next flight and destination.

Zoc - You told them.

Sibi - Yes!Six weeks, but not where.

Zoc - What's on the agenda for tomorrow?

Sibi - I haven't decided yet. Do you have a suggestion?

Zoc - No. They planned today's menu. Let them decide again tomorrow. Maybe something else will develop. In the meantime tell them our flight was cancelled.

Sibi - For how long?

Zoc - Tell them it's pending, maybe a year or so.

Sibi - Setting a trap sir?

Zoc - Not a trap, but rather a game of will. I don't think they're planning anything, but who knows.

In the meantime keep an even tighter rein on them. I want to see what develops.

The next morning Sibi arrives. Heidi answers the door.

Come in, Sibi. Did you talk to Zoc and find out if the next trip is back to earth?

Sibi - All flights have been cancelled for a year or more.

Heidi's eyes well up in tears.

Sibi - I'm very sorry, very sorry.

Heidi - It's not your fault.

Sibi - Think of something else, get your mind off it for a while. Where would you like me to take you today ?

Heidi - I don't know. I just don't know. The other girls were planning an outing without the guys.

Sibi - The men are not going?

No Sibi, replies Heidi.

Sibi - Get your friends then.

Heidi fetches Connie and Lucy.

Heidi - I have some news from Zoc.

Connie - Well?

Heidi - Let's go with Sibi. I'll tell you on the way.

Lucy - Good news?

Heidi - Please let's enjoy today. I promise to tell you both.

John walks in. Hi Sibi, any news...Heidi interrupts... later John.

Sibi - I hear you men aren't going with us?

John - No Sibi...we're going to play cards!

Sibi - Suit yourselves. You girls wait here while I bring the car around.

He telephones Zoc...Commander, the girls are going with me. The men want to stay home. What should I do?

Zoc - Don't do anything to raise their suspicions! Bye.

Sibi drives the car around, picks up the girls...where to?

Upstairs John gets Tom and Paul. We're alone now. Prof. can you get an acid or chemical that disolves steel.

Sure, says the Prof. That's easy if I can find it.

Try your best Prof. See you back here. The Prof. leaves. Now, Tom says John. I have come up with a plan that I think will work. Excuse me one minute. Tom calls downstairs. Yes, came the reply. We need a technician up here. The food dispenser isn't working properly. No, I don't want a waiter to bring food. Just a technician please. Hangs, up. Now we wait.

Tom - Now I'm curious.

Moments later a repairman arrives. What seems to be the problem, sir?

John -I'm not sure. I got a shock when I pushed the button.

Okay, let's take a look. Seems to be working o.k. No shock.

Please pull it out and check it. I don't want my wife to get shocked!

The serviceman pops the front off, takes his meter out.

Checks out one hundred percent ! No problem that I can find. Maybe just a freak surge of some sort.

John - Well thank you for coming. Good day.

Serviceman leaves.

Tom - Now what was that all about.

John - Part of my plan. Last night I kept staring at this thing and it came to me if this unit can be programmed to speak English then we can program a space craft. Get it?

Tom - So far I got it. But with the serviceman?

John - I was looking over the face of the module and couldn't figure out how to open it...serviceman!

Walla!!

Tom - Yes. I was watching him closely, no tools were used. Push down on both sides, twist half turn and out she comes. I'm going to try it. Wow! Easy as pie. Now what?

John - You're the computer designer. I'm the electronic tech. What do you think?

Tom - Now I know why we visited the Space Center. I know exactly what you want.

John - Now I think is a good time to let the Prof, and our wives know what we plan. Remember this is off only if Zoc takes us back to Earth in six weeks.

Tom - We'll ask Sibi if he found out if Zoc's trip is to Earth.

John - If not, Plan "A" in effect. (High five)

There's a lot of small details to work out. If it's a "Go" the girls can help. We can make every second count, check and double check.

Tom - What if Plan "A" doesn't go as planned; Plan "B"?

John - You got it budddy, Plan "B". Tonight when the girls arrive and the Prof, is here, we'll exchange ideas and discuss what everyone is scheduled to do. Both men for most of the day discussed certain possibilities, the shoulds and should nots. Prof, returns mid-afternoon.

Prof. - I've found a shop where they sell items that we need. But I couldn't purchase them. You have to have some identity card or written permission by the Chemical Board.

John - We need these.

Prof. - Since I'm a chemistry professor I'll try the Chemical Co. itself. Just by chance I may get lucky.

Tom - Okay. For now Prof. John and I have worked up a plan and an alternate plan.

John - Let's wait for the girls. I'm just not in the mood to repeat it three times in one day.

It wasn't long before the girls arrived back.

John - Quick girls, we have something important to tell you!

Heidi - First I have something more important to tell you. This morning when Sibi arrived I asked him point blank when are we going home! He replied all flights have been cancelled for a year (her voice begins to falter) or so.

Tom - Eureka, Plan "A"!

Heidi looking very depressed glares at Tom.

John - We all feel your pain, But...

Heidi - Sure! Eureka!

John - We stayed behind today to discuss a way of getting home if Zoc didn't take us back in six weeks.

We came up with a plan...Plan "A". A way to get home on our own.

Heidi - We all want to go home. Are you suggesting we bribe some space cadet?!

John - Nothing like that. I'm talking about us flying a space craft.

Connie - You're joking?

Tom - No, we're not.

Lucy - You're out of your minds!

Connie - I remember your secret talks outside this building so no one can hear you. Now you talk about stealing a space craft and you're not even worried about eavesdropping. Lucy's right. You're out of your minds!

Tom - Maybe so. But listen to the plan first before coming to any decision!

Lucy - Everyone seems to forget Zoc and his generosity.

Tom - No, we thank Zoc for all he's done. But remember this. It's not Zoc who's holding us here. It's the Space Commission who decides when and where we go... not Zoc!

Lucy - Zoc has been very good to us. Yet the Commission may be the only way off this planet. Did you go to the Commission? No, I don't think so! Just your wild scheme.

John - Easy, Lucy, it's not so wild an idea as you may think.

Prof. - Lucy honey, at least hear them out, then decide.

John - How about your Lucy going to the Commission. Find out for sure?

Lucy - I'll have Sibi take me there.

John - Good. Then we can all decide which way to go.

Tom - Then we'll wait till after Lucy gets back.

The following morning when he arrived Tom asks Sibi if he would drive Lucy to the Space Commission.

Sibi - Maybe I can help you?

Tom - We already got your answer yesterday - all flights cancelled. Lucy wants a definite answer.

Sibi - What do you do while I take Lucy over?

Tom - We will wait for your return. I'm sure it won't take a minute or so of the Commission's time for an answer.

Well then, Lucy are you ready?

Lucy - Yes.

After Lucy and Sibi leave.

Tom - What if the Commissioner says one or two years off.

Could we stand to wait that long?

John - If it's a definite date, even if it's two years, we wait. It's much safer than any plan we can come up with. But if nothing is definite, then there's absolutely no reason not to adapt Plan "A" no matter the risk.

Tom - I hate to throw a monkey wrench into this, but if Plan "A" or "B" fail, we all may spend some time in jail!

John - Risky, yes, but failure is not an option!!!

(Lucy returns). Sibi leaves.

Well, came the answer. No scheduled flights to Earth in the foreseeable future. The Commissioner said it may be ten or more years, if then. He said he was sorry. Economics play a big part in space travel. They would send out a craft if it warrants the expense. Something in return if you please.

John - That's that. Well, Lucy, are you with us?

Lucy - I'll help you.

John gives each one a list of what to purchase. The girls had their list, the men theirs. The Prof, still had only the same instruction, thus no list.

That same day the Prof, went to the Chemical Plant outside of town. The girls went their separate ways. John went to the library, Tom to the electronics store. That evening each one staggered in one by one with their items. Most items were obtained the first day. The Prof, was last to arrive.

Prof. - Gentlemen, I have some very good news!

John - You got the acid.

Prof. - No! Something better!

Tom - Well, spit it out!

Prof. - Knowing too well you need a license or a permit, I thought it would be risky, so I applied for a job at the Chemical Plant.

Tom = What about the language barrier?

Prof. - There I lucked out. The manager spoke some English and he gave me a test. I passed and was hired. Start this week. That means I can get my hands on all sorts of chemicals.

John - That's better than I planned. Good, good! Now let's go over the items purchased.

Now that we have Sibi out of our hair for a while, we'll have a good time going over Plan "A" and our alternate Plan "B" if anything should go wrong. John brings out some schematics he had photostatted at the library. Tom brought the electronics. The girls spread out their items, pants, shirts, socks, caps, hoods (all black), stop watches - same brand with second hands plus regular watches, grease paint and an assortment of children's toys. Also binoculars, small pen lights, tape measures, etc.

Heidi - All items make sense except one...why the children's toys?

John - Tom is going to design a robotic toy. I'll wire it up for testing. This way we're sure we can install our own computer or hook up to theirs. But we must be sure of the wiring and workings of their onboard computer. Late into the night John studied the wiring schematics and found most symbols similar to his with small variations. Tom was busy following the schematics with John. Seems relatively easy... let's assemble the toys and get our computer made up and call it a night. Easily said but not so easily done. It was almost dawn when they finished.

John - I'm too tired to test it out.

Tom - I'm pooped too' Let's test it tomorrow.

Both agree and headed for some much needed sleep.

The next day, almost noon now, Tom stirs, gets up.

Connie wasn't around (Tom to himself, she's probably with Heidi). He gets dressed and goes over. (John is awake). Tap, tap. Good morning, buddy. Morning, John says. Tom - Connie here? In the other room with Heidi...

John - Ready for the test?

Tom - Sure! Did you eat yet? Not yet. Let's eat, then test. Okay, replies John.

(Later) The testing goes well. Everything that they programmed in performed exceptionally well. But many more tests were needed. They didn't want anything breaking down. A few of the tests included a vibration test, dropping test. Each time the toy would respond expertly with no exceptions. Programming English into the toy was the most challenging, but with the help of the food processor all worked well.

Now that they knew they could convert the computer into English, the next step was to be the most dangerous of all the plans. A real test...a space craft...an on board computer!

Part one was done...supplies

Part two... computer.

Part three of Plan "A" to commence as soon as possible.

Part three had to be tested on a space craft. If it worked, then on to Part four.

Arrangements were made with Sibi to go out to the Space Center again. Sibi agreed and would pick them up in the morning.

Sibi at once goes to see Zoc repeating to him. He tells of this new trip to the center again. Zoc says so this is the third trip to the center! I've also learned from the Commission that the girl named Lucy was asking questions of their return trip and they told her it may be 10 years or more.

Sibi - Yes, I took her but I didn't inquire about her visit.

Zoc - Every day I get the vouchers back to be paid. Most of them are okay. I received several today which are most questionable - four stopwatches, binoculars, black clothes for all six. They are definetly up to no good. Once I know a little more, then I'll act.

Sibi - In the meantime are there any specific orders other than keeping an eye on them?

Zoc - I ask too much of you to act alone; take along Tollo. He can help watch them. They're more cunning and adaptable than I realized. Two can play this game.

The following morning Sibi arrives with his fellow companion. Good morning everyone. This is my friend, Tollo. He'll be going with us.

After the introductions they headed for the Center.

Sibi - I see you're carrying cameras and what's in that box?

John - The box...extra food so we don't have to stop.

Sibi - This is the second time we're here. There are other places you haven't seen yet.

Tom - Back home John and I visit the airport quite often. We love aircraft. Sibi - So it would seem.

Tom - We randomly have the girls pose and take snap-shots.

John - Goes aboard one of the craft with Heidi. Tagging along is Tollo.

Heidi distracts Tollo by breaking her string of pearls. Oh, mercy me, cries Heidi as the pearls roll all over.

(John sees his chance and opens the box, takes out the food processor and hides it behind a locker). Meantime Tollo is busy helping pick up the pearls.

(Heidi winks at John).

Tollo - I think we have most of them. Heidi thanks Tollo for his help and puts the loose pearls in her purse. Tom and Connie are at the Control Tower, Tom still taking pictures mostly of locks and security systems. Sibi doesn't suspect Tom as Tom always has Connie posing in the pictures.

Sibi notices the Prof, and Lucy must have slipped out; maybe they're with John and Heidi he thinks to himself.

Sibi - Where's the Professor and his wife?

They must be with John and Heidi!

Sibi - We have to find them.

Tom - Okay, we'll wait here.

(Sibi is not sure what to do now; should he leave them and look for the other two and possibly lose Tom and Connie too?)

Tom - Go ahead or stay here. I'm sure they're not lost (thinking to himself).

I know they are not lost but Zoc said to keep a close eye on them.

Tom - Sibi...Sibi...we lost you for a while. Are you going or staying?

Sibi - Oh, yes! Just thinking to myself. I'm sure they are with your friends and Tollo.

While Tom is taking more pictures Connie is pacing off the distance from one sector to the other. Every so often she would excuse herself and head for the ladies room and transcribe her notes to paper.

Sibi - She sure uses the ladies room a lot.

Tom - Too many drinks last night and today. Can't hold it.

Meanwhile the Prof, and Lucy check the door locks, timing devices and entry locks for crafts. Plus the location of all switches.

It was a nerve-racking day for the six not being sure if they were detected; also if they got all the needed information. The time to find out was tonight when they compared notes.

The sun was starting to go down now and you could see the two moons. They headed back - the group to the apartment and Sibi and Tollo to Zoc's home.

At Zoc's Apartment

Well, you two, what have you found out?

Sibi - For one the Prof, and his wife slipped out on me.

I thought they may have been with John and Heidi, but they weren't. Tom took so many rolls of film I couldn't count. And his wife...I don't think it amounts to much, but she was constantly using the ladies room.

That's not much to go on says Zoc, but I'm wondering what the Prof, and his wife were doing? In any case, what did you notice Tollo?

Tollo - Well, Sir, I was with John and Heidi aboard one of the space crafts when Heidi's necklace broke and her pearls ran all over the place. While picking up the pearls I noticed John hide something behind a locker.

Zoc - What was it?

Tollo - Never checked. I'm just reporting to you what I found or saw.

Zoc - It's dark out now but I want you to take me to the Center and show me what John hid.

Later That Evening

This is the craft Commander Zoc, says Tollo. Tollo shows Zoc the locker. Zoc reaches behind the locker, brings out the food module.

That's from the apartment. He puts it back behind the locker.

Tollo - Why did you put it back Sir?

Zoc - Never mind! Take me back to my apartment.

The following day Zoc visits the Space Commission.

Gentlemen, says Zoc. I have been shadowing the Earthlings and I'm quite certain that they are planning to steal one of our space crafts and head for home.

Are you quite sure Commander?

Without a doubt replies Zoc.

They are your responsibility Commander, but we could intercede if you're absolutely sure. If you are wrong then you and this Commission would be in serious trouble with the Government. I'm leaving it up to you and your men to catch them in the act. Then and only then can or will we interfere. Until then, Zoc, you're dismissed.

Zoc contacts Sibi.

Sibi, says Zoc, if you were going to steal a space craft, when would you do it?

Probably late at night, when there's no moons!

Zoc - Then we both agree on a dark night! When is the next date we have for a moonless night?

Sibi - According to the calendar six (6) weeks from tomorrow. That makes it the third week of Autumn. We have less than five weeks to plan. Now here's what we do.

John to Tom...It looks like the best night of the year here, no moons! We'll have to go back to the Space Center one more time before then.

Tom - Just you and me?

John - Yes, we have to hook up the computer and run some tests.

Tom - That's awful risky!

John - I know, but we have no choice. Although our toy models worked, we can't take a chance that it may not be accesible to the on-board computer.

Tom - I agree. It may not work once we hook it up.

It's a big gamble and a big risk.

John - Just pray to God that we can pull this off!

# Chapter 7

## *Change of Heart?*

Well Sibi, I was thinking our plan is sound, but I may have another solution, says Zoc. What might that be, Sir?

Zoc - I thought if we could convince the earthlings that our world is the most productive and the safest planet in our solar system, they may decide not to return home. Set up a meeting with them for tomorrow.

Tom - Zoc's coming over today. For what purpose inquires John.

Tom - Sibi didn't say, but we have to hold it in the Prof.'s apartment.

John - Yes, we don't want him to see the missing modules!

You know John, says Tom. He's on to us.

John - I'm sure of that, but we're on to him too.

Tom - Sort of cat and mouse. John - We're still committed!

Tom - Not unless he's coming over to arrest us.

John - One thing to assume, but still another to prove!
Buzzer rings

Tom goes to the door, looks at Zoc, and into the hall. (He's alone, good).

Come in Zoc says Tom. What did you want to see us about?

Zoc - Just a little visit, that's all.

Tom - Why don't we all go over to the Prof.'s pad.

Fine, says Zoc.

John gets Heidi. Tom calls Connie. We're going to the Prof.'s place. All right, came the reply. Now that we are all here I'd like to tell you about Anfora. As you know we speak many languages. This you know. Four thousand year's ago when we first started exploring the heavens we discovered your planet. At first we thought it uninhabited so we landed. To our surprise it was. The earthlings were very primitive. We made some friends. We showed them little things such as what a plumb line was used for, how to make bows, etc. They in turn thought we were Gods. This was not our intent. We had to leave. We wanted to inhabit, we didn't. We could have been Gods and we wouldn't. Through the eons we finally picked up your radio waves, later on television broadcasts. You were slowly becoming of age. But Anfora decided not to go back until there was an understanding between your Nations. We never would have contacted you this time. It was quite by accident. We had learned your language from broadcasts in the hope that someday, within our lifetime, to finally make an official first encounter. We on Anfora have learned to get along with our neighbors, keep the environment clean, green and pollution free. We succeeded.

Please ask me some questions.

Prof. - Do you have atomic energy?

Not at the present.

Prof. - Why not?

We have not as yet to have atomic energy without nuclear waste. Therefore, until we come up with fission with no by-product, we don't use it.

John - Do you use fossil fuels?

We use oil, but not for heating or automobiles. We use oil only for lubrication, plastic manufacturing and other uses.

John - What about coal?

Not used at all!

John - Why not?

It costs too much to mine, to filter out toxic fumes.

There again it is used only in manufacturing. If we used coal it would in the long run cost us more than it's worth.

Tom - How so?

Many; finding, mining, transporting, environmental clean up plus filters cost money. When these filters are no longer any good, throw them in our landfills? Not here. Make a filter that can be cleaned and used again. No! Chemicals to clean filters? Then how do we dispose of the chemicals? Again, landfills?! NOT HERE.

Tom - Then you only use electric and magnetic?

As you have seen along our highways wind generates our electricity and magnetic power. I should mention water power and solar energy.

John - Earth has never picked up a signal from space. Not even here. How come?

Anfora is located well within your Milky Way. We have many asteroids and the like. If one hit there would be a catastrophe. We needed some protection in the event that it could happen...hence our scientists came up with a solution. Enhance our outer ozone area with a magnetic pulse, thus no signal can pass through and nothing can go out.

John - What about a meteor (10) ten miles across?

It would penetrate! Of course, here on the planet we would get the shock wave. This could cause damage of an enormous scale. But Anfora would be saved.

Prof. - How can you pick up radio waves and such if you have this magnetic pulse and how do you contact your space vehicles?

There we have satellites orbiting well above the magnetic pulse and field receiving signals and passing them both ways.

Prof. - I still don't understand; would you be more specific?

When a signal passing in either direction is received or sent, it's broken down to a frequency well above the human ear and sent through the pulse at certain intervals in conjunction with the receiver set to the same pulse and frequency, thus MAGNETIC PULSE! In other words, it's in sync with the pulse.

Heidi- On one of our excursions Sibi said the buildings and roads were made of the same material. Yes, you thought it was stone?

Heidi - I suppose.

It's a manmade material, carbon base, stronger than titanium and five times lighter. Not only used in buildings and roads, it also encases our space craft.

Tom - How are your space crafts propelled and at what speed?

We have three types of propulsion; electro-magnetic, ion and proton. Proton is the fastest craft we have followed by ion and last electro-magnetic. The electro-magnetic travels eighty-seven thousand miles per hour. Ion approximately ninety-seven thousand miles per hour. And the proton engine can exceed the speed of light (how fast is classified).

John - Wait a minute. According to our scientist (Albert Einstein) nothing can exceed the speed of light. Yes, that is what you learned on earth. I know the theory. But he was wrong.

John - When you approach the speed of light, if I remember correctly, you gain mass, therefore, more fuel is needed.

Basically, says Zoc.

John - A catch-22?

I'm not familiar with this statement, says Zoc.

John - Not important.

Another thing I should tell you and that is you came to Anfora by a proton engine, replies Zoc.

Prof. - To the tune of faster than light!

Tom - Just how far is Earth to Anfora?

Approximately one hundred light years away.

John - That means we've traveled on your craft for a hundred years?

Zoc - That is correct.

John - I don't buy it.

Zoc - You're here, yes?

John - That we are bat that would make us all one hundred years old. Plus the age at the time we came aboard!

Zoc - Your addition is good, But your understanding is not,

Tom - Please explain then,

Zoc - I was about to. Now, says Zoc, the faster you go in space (compared to your friends on Earth) is known as space time. On Earth time is a steady rate, while time is always changing in space according to the rate of time in space.

John - It's beginning to make some sense but we'll still age, right?

Zoc - I'll try to explain this a little better. Let's see...ah... the faster you go the slower the time. When you reach the speed of light, time stands still.

Tom - Okay, I get it, time stands still. How does this affect us, we still move?

Zoc - It does to some extent.

Tom - How so?

Zoc - On board a space craft travelling the speed of light passengers and crew are still moving; but at a much slower rate.

Tom - You mean we are in slow motion?

Zoc - Precisely. Therefore, traveling at 100 light years would appear to those aboard that they have only been aboard a short period of time.

Prof. - Then anyone you knew before you left on such a journey would be long dead before you came back.

Zoc - Absolutely.

Prof. - What of your Government?

Zoc - Hopefully,after a round trip equaling two hundred light years can be nerve racking, not knowing if your world you know when you left will still be there when you return.

John - That's spooky!

Prof. - By the way, what's your crime rate on Anfora?

Zoc - Throughout our society and most of our world, the crime rate, including murder, extortion, robbery, blackmail, etc. etc. is less than two percent.

Prof. - That's amazing!

Zoc - We cannot stop all crimes, this is impossible. But since most countries under the leaders of our world try to maintain a workable wage in conjunction with the other countries, we manage to have a balance of security. Yet some are not satisfied. Anfora nature as it is cannot stop all crimes. No country is jealous of his neighbor, thus there are no super powers.

Tom - Do you retain an army or navy?

Zoc - We have a very small force. Anfora has a standing force including all three; army, navy, air force totaling no more than three thousand, which as far as I am concerned is far too many troups.

John - When was your last war?

I'm not sure about the true date, but it was well over two thousand years ago.

Zoc - Connie, you and Lucy haven't asked questions?

Heidi - I can't think of anything more to ask.

Connie and Lucy - asks Zoc.

No, says Connie.

Me either replies Lucy.

Well then, says Zoc. I guess that's it. If you can think of something later on, don't hesitate to call on me.

(Zoc leaves).

Back at his apartment he calls Sibi...stop over this afternoon. I want to discuss the earthling meeting.

(Meanwhile back with the group). Tom looks at John and the Prof.

Tom - Well, what do you make of that?

Prof. - I think he's trying to persuade us to take another look at his world through his eyes.

John - He knows or thinks he knows our plans. Maybe it's his way of persuading us to stay.

Tom - I agree with both of you and he's trying very hard. After today's session I know he knows.

Heidi - Now you've got me scared.

John - As I said before, he may suspect, he may even know, but can he prove it!

Tom - Heidi has a valid excuse to be scared. We all are.

John - Naturally.

Tom - We should test the module before we take off, but know it seems too risky. Why not install it the night we leave?

John - You could be right. Why take chances and get caught, then everything we planned for goes down the drain.

Tom - The night we are ready to go and the module doesn't work we can come back here and nobody's the wiser.

John - That's if we're not caught!

Prof. - We never considered this space time into our plans ! Now what?

John looks at the rest of the group and says the Prof, has made a point here that maybe we should reconsider our options. A trip back means that things on our world may be quite different when we return. Will America still be a super power or a third world nation under some other nation...etc.

(A long pause).

Heidi is the first one to respond. I still want to go home.

John - I stay with Heidi no matter what!

Connie - I go or stay. It's up to Tom!

Tom - We're with you two.

John - Well, Prof, that leaves only you and Lucy?

Prof. - I'll help you get home, but I've already talked to Lucy about going home. She loves it here and I have a job here that pays me more than I could ever earn at home. Therefore, we have decided to remain here.

John - We stand by your decisions and we do appreciate you helping us. I'm just sorry you won't change your minds.

Tom - We're all going to miss you two.

The girls all embrace as tears cascade down their cheeks.

Lucy - Our best of wishes and luck to you in case we don't get a chance before the night you leave.

Zoc had no idea how his lecture would affect the outcome. Little did he know that at least he had persuaded one third of the group.

(At Zoc's apartment).

Sibi arrives.

Come in Sibi.

Sibi - How did the meeting go?

I told them many things about our world and they asked questions. Still I'm not sure if I got to them or not. They may or may not have a change of heart.

Sibi - So what do we do now?

Zoc - Same as before, watch them, especially those two dark nights. I still believe if they are planning to leave it's on one of those two nights.

Sibi - Do we follow them?

Zoc - No, we go those two nights and wait in the space craft where the module is hidden.

Sibi - What if they plan to leave earlier?

Zoc - I'll take my chances on the two nights. Don't forget they bought black clothes and pen lights.

Hopefully after hearing me today they'll reconsider.

I, for one, don't mind spending two nights in the craft for a NO SHOW!

Sibi - Then you'd have won them over!

Zoc - That's my wish. A no show.

# Chapter 8

## *Burnwell*

The year July tenth, two thousand thirty-eight (2038) A gala celebration was to be held the following day for the retiring Calvin Burnwell, Sheriff of the City of Stratton. Cal had been Sheriff for more than forty years. Now the celebration was a tribute to his many years of dedicated service. They were making their final preparations. School bands rehearsing, floats and the Mayor going over tomorrow's speech. Vendors would be selling pennants, balloons, food, etc. A large banner was strung across the main street (Good Luck to Our Cal). In short, it was to be the biggest affair ever.

(At the Burnwell House)

Sarah was thinking back when she first met Calvin. Cal was in one of her classes in high school. She noticed right away that he was something special. He would stare at her and she would pretend she didn't notice. She had many occasions to get Cal in a conversation, but he was very shy, or maybe he didn't like her? A close friend told her that her first instinct was correct. That summer Cal was elected by a large margin (82%) and soon after taking up his position as Sheriff of Stratton. He asked Sarah if she would work for him as Secretary and Dispatcher. She was thrilled and accepted the position. It was soon after that that the group of vacationers disappeared.He was running here and there. Finally the search was called off.

After a month Sarah decided to ask Cal out. It worked soon Cal was asking her to go here and go there. She loved Cal and hoped he would ask for her hand. Cal did ask her to be his wife. He admitted he'd been in love with her since high school. A year later they were wed. The following year Sarah gave birth to a baby boy, they named him James, Jimmy for short.

Hi Honey! I'm home cries out Cal. Sarah - In here Cal.

Well, says Cal, One more week untill full retirement and then we can go on a vacation.

Sarah - Where to?

Cal - wherever you wish! Jimmy can take over my job!

Sarah - He's not elected yet.

Cal - The polls show him way out front. Let's not count our chickens" replies sarah. Cal by the way how was your day?

Sarah - You woke me out of a reminiscing dream.

Cal - Sorry.

Sarah - I was thinking back to those school days and us.

Cal - All good , I hope?

Cal - That was long ago before I married your Mom.

Jimmy - The paper said in your career you solved every tpye of crime including several murders, assorted roberies, all but one, the missing six vacationers. That's ninety nine per cent!

Cal - Let me see that. Where's my glasses!

Sarah - Your thermos too! Both laugh.

Jimmy - What's funny?

Sarah - some other time Jimmy, Let me read the article

Sarah - Look at all these photos, you dear with the dupties, you and me, Lt. Miles and his troups, the town volunteers and so much more, here's one of Len and Andy with me at the switchboard. You Cal with the reporters. Pictures of Mr. Stratton and Red

Cal - The town has certainly changed through the years. I guess that comes with age.

Jimmy -You know dad, (If I'm elected) It's going to be tough filling your shoes.

Cal - Don't worry son you'll win!

Jimmy - Ninety nine percent!

Sarah - No Jimmy! Your dad solved 100 percent of the cases!

Dad's 100% in my book too!

Sarah - Of course, but that's not what I meant. Your Dad did solve the case of the missing vacationers.

Jimmy- I don't get it - they were found?

Sarah - No, but your Dad knows what happened to them. Would you like to take it from there?

Cal - Okay, you heard what your Mother said. Now I'll add what is not known. I retrieved a CD from a video recorder belonging to one of the group. Plus two cameras (the camera you know about). When I was leaving I took one more look around after taking the CD with me. I searched the horses saddle bags; the sand-wiches were not eaten and the canteens were full. I let the horses loose. They knew their way home.

Jimmy - What about the CD?

Cal - I'm coming to that. I put it in my machine when I got back and was interrupted by Lt. Miles. It wasn't until several days later that I remembered the CD.

Sarah went to get the CD to show Jimmy. Be right back says Sarah. Ah, now watch this.

Jimmy - A spaceman! Well, well. Then it is 100 percent.

Sarah - I told you.

Jimmy - Wait til I tell the paper.

Sarah - Just hold on, it's our secret!

Jimmy- But why? It'll make you famous.

Cal - Do you know why it's a secret?

Jimmy - Why?

Cal - First, if I told them they would call me a liar. Second, if I showed the CD they'd say I'd concocted it. Third - they would ask me why I didn't show it before the search began.

Fourth, I'd have to admit I'm absent-minded. Fifth - Look at the overtime paid out to the deputies, not to mention the National Guardsmen, Lt. Miles to the copter. Plus all those people (volunteers) helping. I thought about this for some time and your Mother agreed to let this be the mystery of Stratton.

Jimmy - I see your point! I'll keep this a secret as long as I live, that's an oath I swear to you and Mom.

Sarah - After your Dad and I are no longer in this world, it would be okay to show and tell what you know today.

Jimmy - I only hope to be as good a Sheriff as you, Dad, if I'm elected.

Cal - You will be, son, you will be.

# Chapter 9

## *The Big Night*

Arrangements had been made to be taken to within two blocks of the Center. They would walk the rest of the way (in case they were being followed). After paying the fare and watching him drive off, they looked around, no one in sight (so far, so good). Hoisting their bags to their shoulders they synchronized their watches and moved out. Ever leery of the unseen eye. Approaching the first objective, a line shack just inside the Center. They all stayed behind while the Prof, left for the shack. They waited for the signal...one blink on the penlite...the Prof, had opened the lock with acid. They hunched over and slowly reached the shack. Once in the shack they quickly donned on the clothes, blackened their faces and attached their hoods. Phase one completed. Phase two was about to commence. Okay, Tom, it's your turn whispers John. You have fifteen minutes. They double-check their watches. I'm off. John taps Tom on the shoulder. Good luck, Budddy! The Prof, peeks out. All clear, go. The center was lit up like a Christmas Tree. Tom had to crawl a good distance before he came to the small ditch which surrounded the southern most part of the field. Still unnoticed he reached the ditch. It was easier going now; he could now proceed faster to the two storage buildings. There he could finally stand up and use the storage building for cover and on to the power station. He checked his watch (making good time). At last the Power Station. Tom takes in a big breath; now to the window he had rigged the last time they were here. Tom looks. A thin wire was attached to the lock that ran outside the window(was it still there he thought?) Yes, it was. He had tested it several times before. Will it still function after so many days? Slowly Tom pulls on the wire. Eureka! It still works. Tom opens the window, climbs in, it was lit up with dim auxilliary lights, not bright at all, just enough that Tom didn't have to pace off the distance as was planned. I'll gain more time this way he thinks to himself. Just then a figure appears and spots Tom. Halt, says the man in Anfora language. Tom lunges at him. They struggle for a minute or two. Finally it's over. Tom knocks him out. But he could come to; must gag and tie him up and finish up what I came for. Looking for something to tie him up with was taking too much time. Using the man's belt, he ties his hands behind him and the man's laces for his legs; then a torn piece of cloth from his shirt for a gag.

Tom broke the seal for the emergency lights first removing a good part of its interior. Next the generators. Reaching into his bag he pulls out three bags (which the Prof, had made up), one for each generator. The trick was to suspend one over each generator, light the fuses and wait. (It seemed like forever). The bags dropped into the generators one by one. There's no explosion, just a grinding sound... some smoke... almost perfectly in sync they stop. All lights, building runway lights, everything went out. Now it was pitch black outside. Tom points his penlight in the direction of the shack...two short blinks! At the line shack, the Prof, with the binoculars spots the signal. He's done it.

John - It's my time to go. Good luck, replies Paul.

Thanks. Now wait for my signal.

Waiting in the space craft Sibi says, all the lights have gone off.

Zoc - Well, it must be a GO for them. I was hoping for a No Show. Right now be still and wait. They'll be along.

John races across the field toward the craft. He hears voices way in the distance. Reaching the craft he enters, turns on the light and heads for the computer on the bridge (thinking to himself, this is it). He pulls out the module and starts installing it. How much time has passed as he looks at his watch. Hum! Three minutes behind schedule; come on hands, work a bit faster for me. Moments later, ahh, now to check it. It certainly would be bad news now if this doesn't work! Crosses his fingers, it's now or never! Computer, do you read me?

Computer - Yes, sir, came the reply.

John - Call me John, okay?

Computer - Yes, John okay!

John - Just call me John!

Computer - Yes, John.

John - Check all your systems and tell me if there's a problem.

Computer - All systems check one hundred percent.

John - Do you have a Star map in your circuits.

Computer - Yes, John, would you like a display?

John - Not now. Do you know where Earth is?

Computer - Yes, John.

John - Then you can take us?

Computer - Yes, John.

John - How far from here?

Computer - 100 light years.

John - That's great.

Computer - Shall we leave now?

John - Not now, later!

Computer - Yes, John.

John returns back down to the entrance. He turns off the lights before opening the ramp door. He peers out (all's clear) takes out his penlight and signals; two short flashes, one long flash.

Prof. - John just signalled, everything is all right.

Tom - Well, that's the signal we've been waiting for. Let's go.

Well, so long you two, I'm sorry you decided to stay.

Prof. - Good luck to you all and God Bless.

Lucy - Goodbye, my very heart goes with you.

Tom - According to my watch we're pretty much on schedule. We're a little behind but not much. You have less than a half hour to get away from here before we take off. And good luck to both of you, too! Prof, and Lucy had changed back into their regular clothes and Tom put all their things in his bag before John had signalled. So they were ready to go.

Prof, and Lucy waved as they moved away.

Their gone now; we'll never see them again.

Heidi - I just hope and pray that Zoc doesn't find out they helped us.

Tom - Don't worry about them. The Prof.'s one smart cookie.

Connie - When do we head for the ship?

Tom checks his watch - twenty minutes. But we can start for the craft now just in case there's anyone out there looking around.

Four minutes later they enter the craft and secure the latch. Penlight in hand Tom searches for the lights. Ahha. Let there be light.

Heidi - What are you doing? They'll see the light and come running.

Tom - No, they won't. Remember Zoc said you can see...

Heidi - Out, but no one can see in. I remember.

Heidi - I'm just jumpy!

Tom - Come on girls, up to the control deck.

John sees them coming down the corridor. In here, gang! Did the Prof, and Lucy get off okay?

Tom - Yes and before they left they wished us luck.

John - We may have to alter our schedule a bit.

Tom - Why?

John - Look out there, a lot of traffic milling around and flashlights too.

Tom - You mean leave now.

John - The sooner the better.

Computer - Yes, John?

Everyone is aboard, you may proceed to our destination.

Computer - Understood John.

They slowly lifted off the surface with the wings extended; they moved faster and faster until they were above Anfora heading for deep space.

Computer - Everything is secure, John.

John - Then proceed at full speed.

Computer - As you wish, John. (It was no time at all when Anfora was no longer in sight).

John - Computer, your other commander on this flight is Tom.

Computer - May I speak with Commander Tom?

Tom - A Commander! I like that stuff.

John - Don't let it go to your head. Tom grins.

Tom - Hello, computer.

Computer - Welcome aboard Commander Tom stuff.

Tom - No stuff.

Computer - No stuff? I'm confused?

Tom - Just Commander Tom.

John turns to Tom. Both of us have to clarify our questions or we could be here forever correcting our orders or questions.

Tom - Why not give our computer a personal name?

John - Good idea. It would be much simpler. Any suggestions?

Tom - Girls...John?

Finally Connie picks out a name...Babe.

Anyone else? Nobody responds.

Tom - With no other names submitted then Babe it is.

John - Computer we have chosen a personal name for you!

Computer - Thank you John.

John - We didn't give you your name yet. First the name, then your thanks. Understood?

Computer - I understand. What is my personal name?

John - Babe.

Computer - Personal Babe, I like it!

John - No, just plain Babe.

Computer - Just Plain Babe, I like that too.

John - Computer!

Computer - Yes John, is there anything wrong?

John - Everything is all right. You are called Babe.

Computer - Babe is very nice. Thank you.

Babe? Yes, John.

John - Nothing at all, just checking. That's all for now Babe. Good night.

Babe - Good night John.

Tom - That was a most impressive demonstration of technology I've ever witnessed.

John - We both did very well in converting it over.

Connie - Tomorrow I'd like to talk to Babe and introduce myself.

Heidi - That goes for me too.

Tom - Well, I don't see why not. What say John?

Fine with me. But remember girls, Babe is a computer and takes in every word. You both have to understand this.

(Back at the Center)

Sibi says, look, one of our craft is taking off. Zoc looks out the portal slamming his fist on the console.

We've been hornswoggledl

Sibi - What!

Zoc - Never mind. Let me think for a while. (Zoc slumps down near the console, elbows resting on the console, fingers going through his hair)....murmuring to himself.

Double duped! Double, double duped. Zoc sat there for some time...suddenly, Sibi!

Sibi - Yes Sir!

We have to contact the commission as soon as possible. Bring the car here.

Pounding on the commissioner's door.

Stop pounding! Come in!

Commissioner, I have some bad news!

Comm. - If it's about the Space Center, I already heard.

This phone has been ringing off the wall. So what's your news as if I didn't know! You're responsible. I told you this before. The Government will not stand for a stolen space craft along with how knows how much technology.

Zoc - Sir!

The Commissioner continues (disregarding Zoc altogether).

They may fire this Commission and dissolve your space career, maybe even jail time for all us us!

Zoc - Please, Sir.

Commissioner - Anything you may have to say may be at your next hearing! Do you read me?

Zoc - You're right Commissioner. That would make it two times in less than four months I'm on trial since I joined the Space Center.

Commissioner - You may very well be tried, but only once.

The first time was just an informal meeting in which you, Zoc, swayed me. But not this time.

Zoc - Commisssioner, I'm guilty as charged. The Commissioner interrupts, Yes, you are.

Zoc - May I continue?

Commissioner - You'll have my full attention for ten minutes, no more. Better make it good!

Zoc - Thank you. As I was about to say, I had them under close surveillance for quite some time when I realized something like this could happen. Lt. Tollo reported seeing John hide a module behind a locker aboard the ship in question.

Commissioner - Two questions, (one) what's this module of which you speak?

(Zoc explains the whole story).

Second, why didn't you contact me at once when you suspected them?

Zoc - No proof. The two darkest night were their best chance of pulling this off. Lt. Sibi and myself along with several others spent the first night aboard this ship to no avail and the second night. That's tonight. They took off in another ship that wasn't being watched.

Commissioner - It seems you were being fooled.

Zoc - These earthlings are very adaptable and cunning.

The phone was ringing again. But no one answered it.

(The Commissioner was calmer now).

You know we're still in trouble! Your Lt. Tollo was supposed to see the earthlings hide the module and report back to you. As you said, Zoc, these earthlings are very deceptive and you fell for the decoy ship!

Amazing, simply ingenious. I see now if you had contacted me they would still be off in space. (Shaking his head)...two modules - who would have guessed?

Commissioner, replies Zoc. There's still a chance!

How?

Zoc - Since the earthlings know nothing of space travel and even less about mapping their way through the galaxy.

Commissioner - You forget one little thing, Zoc ..the computer does!

Zoc - Exactly. They can't compute a course...they can only rely on the computer.

Commissioner - Go on.

Well, they took the very same ship they came here on.

It left here on assignment to collect specimens. No direct course was set for Earth. We made two stops on our journey. Nothing was found so I decided to head towards Earth's solar system and try our luck there. If not, we would head home. The good luck is I never deprogrammed the computer when we arrived home.

Commissioner - I can see where your going with this.

Zoc - Sure, even if I left a month from now I'd take the direct route to Earth. I could intercept and regain our craft. That's if it's okay.

Commissioner - In any case they can't put you on trial if you're not here. But you have to leave ASAP before questions start flying.

Zoc - Thanks, Commissioner. You won't regret it.

Commissioner - I'm already regretting it. Now get your crew and make tracks.

Thanks Commissioner, come on Sibi. We have no time to lose.

Three hours later.

Sibi and Tollo had gathered a crew, but told them nothing of their destination or purpose as Zoc requested. Those who came on this mission knew of Zoc's reputation, thus no questions were asked and they were only too glad to explore the galaxy with him. Once zoc had plotted a course he fed it into the computer and they were off.

(Aboard the Earthlings' craft)

Everything they had planned went off with no hitches. The computer had its job and the crew were settling down. Every day passed without incident. They talked about Anfora, the things they experienced and what they saw. Even if their first day back on earth and what it would be like. The girls had fun talking to the computer and even enjoyed Anfora movies. Months passed.

Both girls enjoyed the Observation Deck watching the different planets, moon nebulas and distant star formations came into view then slowly passed on. Connie - Look, Heidi. We're slowing down. At the same moment John and Tom notice the slowing. Babe, says John, Yes, John

Why are we slowing down?

Babe - Scheduled stop, John.

John - Scheduled stop? We have engine problems?

Babe - Commander Zoc programmed me to stop for exploration. We have no engine problems, John.

John - Babe, forget the exploration stop and put our flight back on my schedule.

Babe - You have to change my flight plan, John.

Tom to John - Now what? John shrugs.

John - Can we delete the scheduled stop?

Babe - No, John. Only Zoc can change the flight plan.

John - How long did you stop before?

Babe - We were at this location fourteen hours John.

Tom - After fourteen hours do we continue on our journey?

Babe - Yes, Commander Tom. After fourteen hours.

Tom - Thanks, Babe.

Babe - You're welcome Commander Tom. The girls in the meantime rush back to the Control Room. We're slowing down!

Tom - Seems we have an unexpected stop. We resume in fourteen hours.

Heidi - What! Why?

John - It's okay. Be patient.

Tom - I wasn't expecting any stop. This means if Zoc is following us, and I'm sure he is, then he's fourteen hours closer. And we can't do a thing about it.

John - Babe, scan and see if any craft is in the vicinity.

Babe - There's no craft John.

John - Good, keep us posted if anything appears no matter how far away.

Babe - Yes John.

John - Do you remember some of the things Zoc told us, says Tom?

John - Some of it. Why?

Tom - The discussion he had on the speed of light?

John - Yes, I remember that, why?

Tom - He said you could go faster than the speed of light.

John - Hypothetically, I think.

Tom - Let's ask Babe!

John - Be my guest.

Babe - Yes Commander Tom.

Tom - Did Zoc ever program the craft to exceed the speed of light?

Babe - Never Commander Tom.

Tom - But can it be done?

Babe - It's a theory, but it has never been tried Commander Tom.

Tom - Thank you Babe.

You're not suggesting that we be the first, says John.

Just a thought, replies Tom.

John - Well, get that out of your mind! A theory not tested; it would be insane.

Tom - You're right, of course. But what if Zoc's ship appears, then what?

John - Besides we can't program the computer to move faster anyway. Just maybe he won't show.

Tom - Be reasonable, you know he will sooner or later!

John - We take our chances.

Tom - That's not like you. You usually have something up your sleeve.

John - I don't know Tom, I'm just washed out.

Tom - Of course you are, we all are. But we should put our heads together and come up with something... anything! I for one don't want to spend the rest of my life in an Anforian prison. John - I often think about that myself.

Heidi - Maybe Babe can find a way out of this for us John.

John - Hum! You may have a good idea; it's worth a try.

John - Babe. Babe - Yes John.

John - In a few hours we'll be under way again. Is there a better or shorter route to Earth?

Babe - Zoc has scheduled one more stop after this and then we head for Earth John.

John - Another stop. How long a wait this time?

Babe - One and a half months from now. We stop to explore another planet, time there will be six hours, twenty-seven minutes John.

John - Then can we take a shorter route to Earth?

Babe - No shorter route can be made without reprogramming John.

John - Well, that's that!

Tom - Well, we can relax and forget about an Anfora ship following us.

John - Yeah. He'll be waiting for us!

Heidi - Can we fight him off?

John - This is an exploring craft, not a fighter!

Heidi - I'm only trying to help.

John - I'm Sorry honey, any suggestions are welcomed. Which does give me an idea. Babe?

Yes John.

John - Since we can't change course, can we slow down?

Babe - No John, it's been pro....

John - Never mind. I know, programmed by Zoc.

John - Tom, is it possible to reprogram the computer?

Tom - Delete Zoc's program and reprogram ours. The answer is yes.

John - Good, let's get started.

Tom - You are forgetting one thing. Neither one of us know where we are located. How could we program a destination not knowing the stars?

John - Babe can give us a map.

Tom - It might work...but...

John - But what?

Tom - The time involved. Plus we'd have to shut Babe down.

John - Yes, to shut down Babe we'd drift endlessly in space.

Tom - Right!

Connie - You're both grasping at straws. You're both tired; why not relax and get a good night's sleep.

Maybe by then you fellas will come up with something.

After all, you two worked together and got us off Anfora.

I'm sure you'll come up with a plan.

Days came and went, still no plan was in the works.

Tom - Babe, how long is it now till we reach our next location in months only, not miles.

Babe - The next destination is one month thirteen days Commander Tom.

Tom - Thank you Babe.

John - We just asked her how long. Now you ask again two days later.

Tom - I forgot, I don't remember a lot of things lately.

John - After today let's not make a plan. We can't possibly do anything to be free of Anfora or Zoc. Instead maybe we can reason with him. Put the shoe on the other foot.

Tom - Yes, it could work. Play on his sympathy.

John - Exactly !

Tom - Well, I guess it's as close to a plan as possible.

Heidi - I just thought of something.

John - Go ahead sweetheart.

Heidi - Sibi was beamed down to Earth and we were all beamed aboard.

John - Oh, baby, you're terrific.

Babe - Thank you John.

John - Sorry Babe...Baby not Babe. Baby is a pet name we give our wives, clear?

Babe - Yes John. Sorry.

John - A question. When we reach Earth could you beam all four of us down.

Babe - Yes John.

Tom - Thanks, Heidi. You have just solved the problem. Earth bound, here we come.

John - This calls for a celebration. John picks up Heidi and swings her around.

Tom and Connie are hugging and kissing.

I'm so happy, says Heidi as she starts to cry; Connie joins in.

Tom looks at John and says, Oh, brother.

John grins ear to ear. Yup! They're happy!

John - Let's go down to the galley for food and drink.

Hand and hand they go down.

The six weeks went by and they were now above their last destination and would soon be on their way. No more stops.

Babe - Yes John.

The scanner we have aboard - can it show us a detailed look at this planet as well as people?

Babe - Yes John, but there are no people on this planet.

John - I gather that, but we would like a close-up view of the planet.

Babe - That is possible John.

John - Okay gang, let's go to the scanner, I'm sure you want to see it too.

As they stare at the scanner - My word, says Connie.

It's so delolate. Reminds me of Mars or the moon.

No wonder Zoc didn't spend too much time here says Tom.

John - Maybe so Tom, but it is interesting to look at, don't you agree?

Tom - Well, it's something we can tell our children and grand-children.

John - Too bad we didn't bring a camera with us. But Tom took many pictures on Anfora.

Tom - I left them behind.

Connie - Oh, Tom!

Tom - Had no time to pack them, besides I had enough stuff to tote.

John - Hello Commander Tom stuff.

(Everyone laughs).

Connie - I was just thinking what Zoc will do when he finds his craft missing of crew.

Tom - Anybody's guess?

They finally left! This time no more stops.

The months just kept going by and they were getting closer to home every day. They did a lot of star gazing.

The last leg of their journey they spent time seeing if they recognized any star formation. No one was versed in astronomy, but they looked anyway. They could have recognized Venus or Mars.

John - Babe, now that we're nearing Earth could you identify anything, anything at all?

Babe - The names of star formations near planet Earth have Anforian names and not translated to English John.

John - Thanks Babe. One thing though. Is Earth in English or in Anfora language?

Babe - Only in the Anforian language John,

John - Then how do you know the word Earth?

Babe - From Zoc. After you came aboard Zoc referred to you as Earthlings from the planet Earth and entered it in my computer bank. Is that all John?

John - That's good. Thank you Babe.

Babe - You're welcome John.

Tom - When you pick up Earth in your scanner, no matter how far away, please let us know.

Babe - Yes Commander Tom.

Heidi - When we reach Earth and we beam down and Zoc isn't waiting for us what happens to this craft?

Tom - Don't worry about the craft or Zoc and his crew.

He'll be here waiting or will turn up sooner or later.

John - Remember Zoc's ship is already programmed to return after we were picked up.

Now look, says John. We only have one thing to do and that's get home. Let's not put any more "what ifs" in this. Leave well enough alone and be ready to beam down when the time arrives.

No more "ifs, ands, or buts", were discussed. It was now just waiting and biding time.

It was too long a wait when Babe announced she picked up Earth on her scanner.

# Chapter 10

## *The Encounter!*

It's still quite a distance away, can't seem to make out much, says Tom. Just a small dot.

John - Babe, let us know when we're closer and can receivie a little more detail.

Babe - Yes, John.

Heidi - At this speed it shouldn't be too long from now.

Connie - I can't wait to get back home again. (Sniffles) It wasn't long at all as Connie had said. Just then Babe announces space craft ahead. They rush to the scanner; all eyes peer out...yes...it's Zoc. I'm sure of it, says Tom.

John - Babe, can you make out the craft?

Yes, replies Babe. It's a Class Two from Anfora.

Connie - Now we're in for it! John - Babe? Babe - Yes, John?

John - Can we avoid Zoc's craft by beaming down before we get too close to him, say from here?

Babe - Too far out, John.

John - How close to Earth before we can beam down?

Babe - Ten miles above Earth, well below where Zoc's craft is waiting.

Not much of a chance of slipping by Zoc's craft, says Tom to John.

John - We have only one choice. Wait on the pad. Zoc's ship is stationary and waiting. At our speed we could pass Zoc's ship and at the right moment beam down.

Babe - Less than thirty minutes out, Commander Tom.

(The girls are huddled together) and just in seconds Zoc appears on the bridge with Sibi and Tollo.

All stood motionless as Zoc stepped forward. They all stared at each other...not one word was spoken. Zoc stood over them like a cat ready to pounce, Heidi shaking as if she were immersed in a tube of ice. She slowly raised her arm and waved it across her face.

What's up Zoc?

Connie giggles...Tom and John couldn't hold back their laughter any longer. Ha, ha, ha, ha Connie and Heidi join in. Finally Zoc couldn't help but laugh himself.

John finally said (still holding back a snicker or two), sorry Zoc, it's a private joke. I know we're in deep shit here.

Zoc - I had to laugh too! But as you say, you're in up to your eyeballs. Deception, sneakiness, destruction, robbery and assault! What do you think you would do in my place?

Tom - There's an old Indian saying on Earth..."Don't judge a man until you have walked in his moccasins for a day".

Heidi - Please Zoc, we love our world as you love yours!

I'm reversing your question - what would you do in our place?

Zoc - Off the record, I'd do the same. Although I don't know if it would be as clever as you six...six...by the way, where's Paul and Lucy?

Connie - They didn't want to come with us.

Zoc - But he's part of this.

John - The Prof, and Lucy knew nothing of our plan.

Zoc - That's hard to believe. Your friend Connie just said they didn't want to go!

John - Sure, we asked them the night of the flight we left and as friends they said they would keep it a secret.

Zoc - Come on now, you just added liar to the rest of the charges!

Heidi - You have a very shallow outlook on humanity.

Zoc - Can't blame me for what happened to you or what I think. You made me the scapegoat in your devious plan. Never even considered what the consequences would be after you left Anfora, did you?

John - I'll be truthful, no! The only thing on our minds was home, home, home and nothing mattered but home, period.

Bravo says Tom!

Zoc - I, too, must admit that in my whole career I have never (including Anfora people) met a more fascinating, brilliant and creative people than yourselves. John - Does that mean you'll give us a break?

Zoc - There are some advantages for me to beam you home, but that may be a problem and... John - What kind of problem?

Zoc - I wasn't finished and if I took you back it could be a different kind of problem.

Tom - What are they?

Zoc - If I beam you down to Earth you don't realize how long you've been away. You left Earth in nineteen seventy-three. You've traveled over 200 light years round trip. That makes the date now on Earth twenty-one seventy-five (2175). Every one you've known is long since deceased. What may lay ahead is also unknown. Your government may not be in power any longer... shall I go on?

John - It's over two hundred years?

Zoc - Yes.

John - Your government may also be gone?

Zoc - Each time I leave Anfora I wonder if it will still be there. But think of this...if you come back with me you can be pretty sure that they will not prosecute. After all, time heals all wounds. Most likely it will be long forgotten.

Heidi - You're giving us a chance to choose?

Zoc - Why not!

Heidi - I'd still like to go home, but now you've got me wondering what's down there. Is America still Number One?

Zoc - One way to tell.

Computer...no response.

Computer...what the...says Zoc?

John - Sorry Zoc, we gave the computer a name. We call her Babe.

Zoc - ? ?Babe?

Yes, Commander Zoc.

Zoc - Well, at least you remember my name.

Of course, Comander Zoc, replies Babe.

Zoc - I'm putting in a new direction.

Babe - Where to Commander Zoc.

Zoc - I'll take over for now, Babe.

Yes, Commander Zoc.

Okay, says Zoc. I'll pilot it down closer to the surface for a better look. Stand by everyone, we're going down.

All gaze into the scanner. Soon they were breaking through cloud cover.

Zoc - Babe, where is the area we picked them up?

Babe - Exact location as before, Commander Zoc.

Heidi - It...it can't be...no trees, nothing, a wasteland.

Zoc - Hang on...Babe check. Are we in the same area as before?

Babe - Exactly Commander Zoc.

Okay everybody relax. Something must have happened replies Zoc.

John - What happened here Babe?

Babe - Unknown John.

Zoc - How far from the town were you, John?

John - No more than four miles give or take.

Okay, let's look around. What direction is the town?

John - West.

Scanning the town of Stratton...barren...nothing but rubble everywhere...no people...no animals. A few green shrubs dotted some of the landscape.

Zoc - Well, we can't beam you down there!

Heidi - Then could you beam us home to Pennsylvania? That's about (2000) two thousand miles northeast of here.

As the craft travels east bound all eyes scan the world below them. It's the same all over the country. What the HELL happened?

Zoc - I'm taking us up to get a better view of the Earth as a whole. I'm going down on occasion to have a more detailed look around the globe. No signs of life. It was the same in every direction. What now?

Babe - Yes, Commander Zoc.

John - Any sign of RADIATION?

Babe - No, John.

Zoc - How's the atmosphere?

Babe - Highly toxic Commander Zoc.

John says to Zoc, well it leaves out nuclear war. Could it have been a meteor or volcano eruptions?

Zoc - Volcanos! Possibly, but all over the globe?

Meteors or comets are highly unlikely. There is only one way to find out.

Tom - How's that Zoc?

Zoc - Babe, take us to these coordinates. Then stop.

Babe - Yes, Commander Zoc.

Well group, you know now you can't return.

Tom - We're well aware!

Zoc - Babe, have you come up with any information yet?

Babe - The Poles shifted as much as thirty degrees very suddenly, Commander Zoc.

John - What caused the shift?

Babe - It was caused by planetary lineup.

John - Explain, as simply as possible.

Babe - Calculating the effect of gravity by the other planets against Earth's gravity caused excessive pull on the Earth's crust causing oceans to override all continents and setting off volcanos globally. The Teutonic Plates shifted causing buildings to topple, bridges to collapse. This shifting also caused internal disruption; volcanos

erupt, rivers and lakes leave their beds, giant tidal waves; glaciers would cause additional destruction.

Buildings not destroyed by floods or fire appear to have been toppled all in the same direction around the western hemisphere signifies a single event. On the opposite side of the globe trees and buildings are toppled in the opposite direction. Both icecaps also contributed to the flood scenario, John.

Zoc - Babe, can you tell when this occurred?

Babe - It happened during the twentieth century approximately, Commander Zoc.

Zoc - Specific please, Babe.

Babe - The later part of 2012, Commander Zoc.

Well, that's that! says Zoc. It looks like you have no other choice but to return to Anfora. I'm very sorry.

Heidi - Thanks for all you've done for us. We all owe you an apology.

Zoc - Like I said before, I would have done the same thing.

John - All those lost souls!

Zoc - We could hold a ceremony for your people if you like!

John - That would be the least we could do.

(After a brief ceremony)

Zoc calls the other ship...have someone take over for Tolo, I'll remain here with Sibi and half the crew. The earthlings will be with me. Understood commander Zoc came the reply.

Under a new skipper they were told by Zoc to head home.

Zoc's craft would follow shortly.

Sibi escorted both couples to their assigned cabins.

Sibi said they would dine in their cabins for the time being until all crewmen were assigned their jobs aboard the craft. Zoc had said he didn't want them underfoot.

Later on, during dinner, John says to the girls. I ask your forgiveness for all the mess I've gotten you into.

Tom - Hold on...I'm just as guilty too!

Connie - We've been behind you all the way. We still are, nothing's changed.

Heidi - We were friends before all this and will remain friends to the end.

John - Thanks, gang.

Announcement over the intercom (First) speaking Anforian language and repeated in English...Message...secure your stations. All others off duty stay in your cabins and secure.

Commander Zoc.

Tom - Now what?

A knock on the cabin doors!

Zoc peeks his head in. Remain seated and buckle up!

Tom - What's up?

Zoc - Have to get back to the bridge. No time to talk! Buckle up NOW!

Zoc rushes back to the bridge.

John - I wonder what's happening up there.

Heidi - Zoc goes out of his way to make sure that we are protected.

Connie - Zoc for some reason or another has always treated us as his children.

John - Well, buckle up as he says.

Tom - I hope he makes it back to the bridge before whatever it is happens. The gamma ray burst and struck.

The huge craft tumbled and rolled over like a ping pong ball in a wind tunnel. The girls were screaming. They were all tossed back and forth like rag dolls. It lasted it seemed forever.

Sibi came to their cabin. Like the rest of the ship it was in an upheaval. Sibi checked; all four were out cold. He touched each one...good, they all had a pulse.

Sibi - Babe, please send a medical team to the earthlings' cabin.

Babe - Yes, Lt.Sibi, right away.

On being revived they looked at the shambles the cabin was in. Sibi said it's a mess, but we survived. Zoc is on his way.

Zoc comes to the cabin. Glad to see you made it through all this.

Tom - How's the craft, Zoc.

Zoc - The craft seems to be still intact. But we lost contact with the other craft!

John - What happened to them?

Zoc - Babe's been sending out signals for some time now; no response. Plus we lost two crewmen and have quite a few casualties.

John - We can help.

Zoc - Good. We can surely use your help. Just one other thing I should mention.

Tom - What's that, Zoc?

Zoc - We're lost in space!

John - Boy oh boy! One thing after another!!!

Zoc - I've been in worse situations than this. Buck up.

We'll find our way, don't fret! In the meantime you girls can help out in the hospital. You two will work with Sibi and me.

Zoc - John, you're with me, and Tom, you will be with Sibi.

John - What do we do?

Zoc - First and foremost help get the wounded down to the infirmary. Then we salvage what we can of this mess.

Heidi - What can we do to help?

Zoc - For the meantime stay in your quarters until we clear up some of this mess. Then you will be sent for.

The infirmary is the most likely place. But first we need to clear the passage ways, don't want anyone tripping or falling over this debri. we have enough casualties as it is. Work is already underway. It won't be long to clear a path.

Zoc - All stations report damage ASAP.

The calls came in one by one.

Engineering - One dead, six injured.

Chief Electronics Chief dead, three injured and from other areas of the ship an additional eight more. Zoc was dismayed at the loss and injured. Reports stated no outside damage sustained to the integrity of the hull. Interior damage was quite a different story. Small fires were quickly put out. Beams were cut out and replaced. Most of the damage occurred on the bridge.

Zoc - You girls can help in the infirmary as I said before.

Connie - Okay, we know the way!

Zoc - My Chief Electronics man is dead and his assistant is injured.

John - Say no more, Zoc. We'll get right on it. Come on Tom.

John - Babe, what's not working?

Babe - Several things are not functioning, John.

John - Give us a list of the most urgent and work down.

Babe - Understand, John. First, Life Support Systems are down on several decks, fifteen, twelve and twenty-three.

John - Hold that for now.

Babe - Yes, John.

John - Zoc, those decks can be sealed off for now.

Tom - I'll get to work on them, see what's next.

John - Babe - What's next?

Babe - Guidance is out.

John - Anything more urgent?

Babe - The rest is minor. It can wait.

John - Thanks, Babe.

Babe - You're welcome, John.

After six hours life support was returned to the affected decks. John was still working on the Guidance System, most of which was restored.

John - Babe, we need to shut down some sections of the ship's computer that's not absolutely necessary to maintain the ship's function.

Babe - That would be the Entertainment Facility and Game Rooms.

John - Thanks, Babe.

Babe - You're welcome, John.

Tom - I can help you, John.

John - Good. First we're going to use the circuit here and reroute to here. But I need a relay switch.

Tom - What voltage?

John - We can get away with a four volt, but not larger.

Tom - Only one I can find is this one. It's bigger but can be stepped down.

John - Get ready to turn off the Entertainment Center.

Tom - Solders in a resister ahead of the relay. All set. Try it.

John - Here goes nothing. Babe, how's it look?

Babe - Working fine, John.

John - Thanks, Babe.

Babe - You're welcome, John.

John - Let's double check the circuits just to be sure.

Tom with meter in hand, checks out A-okay!

Zoc - You two have been at it for twelve hours straight. Take a break.

Tom - No need...we've finished.

Zoc - I don't know what to say, but thanks, both of you.

Tom - One small hitch though!

Zoc - What's that?

Tom - There will be no entertainment aboard this craft. We had to cannibalize some of its circuits.

Zoc - We can do without (laughs).

# Chapter 11

## *Out There*

Zoc and his crew along with the group were attempting to secure the remaining sectors. Babe was still scanning space trying to spot some constellation that was familiar and sending out signals hoping to find the other space craft. The girls were working in the infirmary, surprised to see Ada again. Zoc held a brief ceremony for his two lost crewmen. After the ceremony they were jettisoned to deep space. Commander Zoc had many problems to solve.

One (1) Food

Two (2) Water

Three (3) Find out where they were.

There was ample food and water aboard for extended journeys, but he knew it wasn't inexhaustible. He had to find a solution or they would all perish.

Months went by with no luck; food and water was getting scarce.

(Over the intercom)

This is Commander Zoc. Starting today all rations and water will be cut by half. That is all.

(No one complained)

More weeks passed, nothing...then one afternoon Babe announced a planet sighted.

Zoc - How far out?

Babe - It will be visual within eighteen hours Commander Zoc.

They all spotted it the following morning.

Orbiting the planet they could see vegetation, rivers and oceans.

Zoc - Babe, what is the composition of the atmosphere?

Babe - Oxygen, Commander Zoc.

Zoc - Any life?

Babe - Yes, Commander Zoc.

(over the intercom)

Attention: As you all know there's a planet below. There is vegetation and water, also some form of life. The form of life is unknown. We are going to land. Zoc out.

Cheers throughout the ship. That same day they landed safely and Zoc assembled a small party to explore and return to the ship as soon as they accomplished their mission.

Those on board who were not on duty were peering out the portal. Look someone cries out...birds, lots of birds.

It's habitable! Easy says one crewman. Let's wait for the away team!

It wasn't long before they came back and immediately reported to Zoc.

Zoc - Well, what's the news? (Heading the party was Lt. Tolo.)

Tolo - Well, Commander, the water was tested...fit to drink.

As for the vegetation, we brought back many varieties including what looks like fruit to be tested...and, Sir, there's birds and animals here!

Zoc - Well done, well done. Get all this down to the lab Not all has to be tested says Lt. Tolo. We watched the birds and small animals eating most of the food we brought back. If they can eat it, I'm sure it's okay for our consumption.

Zoc - still, we'd better check to make sure we can consume it. The animals may have an immunity to any given bacteria or toxins that they can eat...we may not.

Tolo - Yes sir.

Zoc - If the vegetables and fruit you brought back are edible, then we can go hunting for some game. If everything turns in our favor, we can start taking on provisions for our long trek home. It was not long before word of mouth reached every ear of the findings.

Zoc announces; you've heard that we found vegetables and fruit. But don't get your hopes up yet! Although the water is safe to drink, everything else is still up in the air until after it's tested for consumption.

The final word was good. They could eat some of the vegetation and most of the fruit. Wild life was plentiful.

Could they stay on this planet? Definitely, without a doubt!

Zoc had other ideas...loading up with provisions and water in the event that they could return to Anfora. Next step was to obtain small game. They would get twelve different species, one of each to be brought aboard for testing.

Sibi had volunteered to head the hunting party. Tom and John wanted to go also. Zoc gave his permission for Tom and John to join the hunt. Along with the three, fifteen more men were chosen. Since this was an exploring space craft very few arms were aboard. Zoc had the machine shop make some small arms. John and Tom were amazed that the ship carried no arms. What they witnessed was down right primitive; crossbows, spears, traps and the like. The small arms aboard were stun guns, nothing more.

Tom looks at John. Well, John. When in Anfora do as the Anforans do.

John laughs.

Sibi - We're ready to go. Do you two know how to use a lance or crossbow?

John - I think we can manage. After all our great, great, great great grandfathers did! Tom chuckles.

Sibi - You two are something else. Let's go!

John - Follow the leader!

Tom - Why not Red Rover, Red Rover.

Sibi - What are you two taking about?

Tom - Nothing Sibi. Just razzing you.

John - This ought to be good.

Tom - You bet! I feel like a kid again.

The hunt took longer than expected. But after five days they had bagged their twelve specimens and returned to the ship.

Testing was done immediately upon arrival. All samples were tested and fit for consumption. A larger party was sent out to collect as much meat as possible to fill the stores. Water was pumped aboard. All fruits and vegetables were either dried, frozen or canned, all meats salted, dried or frozen. For the most part they lived off the land. All provisions now stored aboard and waiting for Zoc to give the word to make fast for the journey home. Although it was a paradise, it was now time to return home, if possible.

Although this "M" Class planet was a paradise, the vast majority wanted to return home, even if it meant never finding Anfora. Zoc said, in any event we can't find our way home, we could always come back.

Babe had stored in her memory bank the location of the "M" Class planet. Maybe one day another Anfora ship could return and colonize this paradise.

The only chance they may have is to try to return to their last encounter with the gamma burst and take it from there. With any luck they would spot some recognized star that would put them on the right path. As it turned out Babe had received a signal from the missing space craft and notified Zoc. Zoc calling Space Craft Two. A faint answer followed; received one of your probes. How much trouble are you in.

Zoc - Everything fine now. We'd lost our bearings, can you help?

No. Two - It's good to hear your voice, Commander Zoc, and yes, we can help you. We're sending out a signal; tune to three seven three montogams..follow this signal beam. We'll wait here for your arrival.

Zoc - Thanks. Will do!

Zoc - Babe, set course to three seven three montogams.

Babe - Yes, Commander Zoc.

(Over the intercom)

We're going home. Contacted missing craft.

(All the crew cheers)

Weeks passed and Babe reports Anfora ship craft dead ahead.

Four men from the second craft beam over to Zoc's craft. They salute Zoc and Zoc salutes back. Well, says Zoc, glad to see you, Commander Swade. Same here. We thought we lost you. When we left Earth we just missed the gamma ray burst. It was heading your way. I decided to wait where we were until we were sure you would make it. When it was over, your craft was nowhere to be seen. We knew if you were still alive you'd be sending out probes. We, in turn, sent probes in the direction you were last seen. Also radio signals.

Zoc - We managed through the gamma burst with some damage. There were seven injured and two dead.

Swade - I'm sorry to hear of the loss.

Zoc - It could have been much worse.

Zoc goes on to tell Swade of the planet they discovered, with all the trimmings. Zoc was ready now to head home. First he told Swade that he would beam over some of the provisions he had stored aboard from Paradise.

Swade - I still don't know how you came through this.

Zoc - I really don't know! Maybe it had to do with the shape of our craft, or something else! But I do know this; people love mysteries and tend to ignore any so-called explanation.

Swade - As good an answer as any.

Zoc - We did luck out, we found that Paradise Planet I discussed with you.

Swade - Our government will surely colonize this one. It's too bad I never got to see it.

Zoc - You will. Bank on it. Maybe you'll help colonize this planet.

Swade - Sounds good, Zoc, but I'm like you, an explorer, not a settler.

Zoc - You could change your mind.

Swade - I don't think so! But one thing I would like to know!

Zoc - What's that?

Swade - We were all volunteers for this mission and only you know what it was all about? I guessed something when we spotted one of our ships, then you beamed over...?

Zoc - Four earthlings stole my craft and I came back to retrieve it.

Swade - They took your ship?

Zoc - It's a very long story. Sibi can fill in all the details.

Swade - I can't wait to hear this!

Zoc - Babe...

Babe - Yes, Commander Zoc.

Zoc - Locate Lt. Sibi and send him to my quarters.

Babe - Yes Commander Zoc.

(Chime)

Zoc - Enter.

Sibi - Reporting Commander (salutes). Both Commanders return salute.

Zoc - Lt. Sibi, this is Commander Swade.

Sibi - We've already met, Commander Zoc.

Zoc - Fine! Okay, Commander Swade would like to know all about our earthlings. Please fill him in.

Sibi - My pleasure Sir.

Zoc - I'll leave you here with Commander Swade, Sibi. I'm going to the Bridge.

(All salute and Zoc leaves)

On the way to the Bridge Zoc pauses... turns around and heads groups' quarters instead. On arrival he taps at the hatch.

Enter came the reply.

The first one he spots is John. Hello, John , says Zoc.

Well, hello Zoc.

Zoc - I came to talk to you four before we get back to Anfora.

John - Of course Zoc. I'll get Tom and Connie. Heidi, Zoc's here. Okay came the answer.

(John goes to Tom's cabin).

John - Zoc's in my cabin. He wants to talk to us. Tom gets Connie and returns to John's where Zoc is waiting.

Well, Zoc, what did you want to talk to us about?

Zoc - As you know when we reach Anfora you'll all be arrested and I came to offer you some help.

John - We appreciate your help, but I'm guilty as charged.

Nothing you do can help. Thanks just the same.

Zoc - Don't be so sure.

Tom - We hashed this out before. Things look pretty glum for the two of us.

Zoc - I've noticed that both John and you take full responsibility. What about the girls?

John - Women are compelled by our laws to follow their spouse under penalty of law!!

Zoc - I'll do my very best for the girls as well as you men, But don't give me that under penalty of law CRAP! Don't forget we on Anfora know your language and laws. We are not naive. Now let's, for once, be honest with each other.

Heidi - Zoc, I never heard you raise your voice before.

Zoc - I apologize, but John sometimes gets to me.

Heidi - John, please, no more far out tales. Tell Zoc the truth.

John - Okay, Zoc. I'm very sorry, but you do know I love Heidi more than life itself. We're in your hands!

Zoc - Good, good! As you know I'm well off and can afford the best of everything. The best lawyer will be at your disposal when we arrive. Sibi and myself will stand as character witnesses for you. What the outcome will be is unknown. But I do know this; time does heal all wounds as I've said before, our laws are fair. As far as I'm concerned you never broke any laws until that night and only because you wanted to go home. Going home is no crime. An all woman jury would eat this up.

John - Just one thing!

Zoc - And?

John - The Professor and Lucy.

Zoc - They were left behind and probably have already been tried.

John - Is there any way to find out their outcome?

Zoc - I'll radio ahead and find out. Remember this; the girls worked in the infirmary with Ada helping my injured crew. And you two helped gather fruits/vegetables, then went hunting, not to mention repairing of the computer.

This must be taken into consideration.

Tom - It may not be as bad as it seems.

Zoc - Exactly.

Connie - Thanks in advance Zoc. We owe you much.

Zoc - Well, I must report to the Bridge. That's where I was heading before I stopped by here. See you all later.

By the way, we're having a celebration of our rescue and the discovery of the new planet tomorrow afternoon. In the meantime, dinner in the Main Hall at (6:00 p.m.) six. By all.

(In unison, bye Zoc. Thanks.)

Babe - Yes, Commander Zoc.

Send a message to Headquarters. Would like information on the earthlings Professor Paul Burrows and wife ASAP.

Babe - Yes, Commander Zoc.

(Four weeks later)

Received message from Anfora to Commander Zoc. Zoc - Thanks, Babe. Please make a printout. Babe - Yes Commander Zoc.

To Commander Zoc
Message as Per Request
concerning Professor Paul
Burrows and wife as follows:
,,,,,,,,,,Charges,,,,,,,,,,
Three Generators Damaged
One Destroyed Lock

,,,,,,,,,,,,
Professor Paul Burrows
Guilty as Charged

| | |
|---|---|
| ,,,,,,,,,,One Hundred Fifty Dollars for Removal of Resin from Generators | $150.00 |
| Two Dollars for Replacement Lock | $ 2.00 |
| Subtotal | $152.00 |
| Court/Legal Fees | $250.00 |
| Grand Total | $402.00 |

No Charges Filed against Lucy Burrows
Professor Paul Burrows paid fine and was released
Anfora Base Commander
Space Center - Commander Tromgolt
Thanks, Babe says Zoc.
Babe - You're welcome Commander Zoc.
Zoc rushes down to see the group.
(Raps on hatch)
Come in says John.

Zoc - Hi, John, received communication from Anfora Space Center. Here, read this!

John - Fantastic...Heidi get Tom and Connie in here!

They all read the communication jumping up and down. Okay, Professor!

Zoc - I'm very glad you're pleased.

Heidi - Oh, Zoc. It's great news. Thank you. Thank you, Connie - Zoc, you're wonderful. The boys put their hands out. Shake Zoc.

Zoc - Put aback (shrugs) but offers his hand. Smiles.

Zoc - I hope it goes as well for you as it did for the Professor.

Tom - I just hope it goes as well too!

Zoc - Hold that thought, all of you.

John - This calls for a celebration.

Zoc - I'm afraid that'll have to wait. We just had a celebration. Now we have to get back to work. Celebrate later. You're all back on duty in less than an hour.

The group was working extra hard replacing eighteen men still in the hospital. Tom and John were shuffled from one part of the ship to the other taking up the slack that was left behind. And the girls were tending the wounded. Washing and ironing were just a few of their tasks. When the day ended they headed back to their quarters. They found they were too tired to celebrate. Day after day the same routine.

Months later things began to change. Some of the wounded returned to duty thus taking some of the load off. Things were getting better now and the group was able to relax a little.

Zoc was very pleased with the way they pitched in and never complained. Zoc thought to himself of raising his voice and calling them everything he could think of, but for every negative thought he'd said to them he had many more positive reasons to like and admire about them. Capability, intelligence, stamina, hardworkers, challenges and so much more. Maybe the Anforians and himself had misjudged the earthlings? But it was too late! Earth was gone. What will become of them once we reach Anfora...

(Zoc was shaken from his thoughts) Commander Zoc, to the Bridge. On my way, replies Zoc.

That day, after the groups tour of duty was over they headed back to their quarters.

Heidi - It's been quite a while since Zoc brought us the communicate. I still wonder now and then how they are?

John - I'm afraid their both deceased by now.

Heidi - Yes, I keep forgetting the time difference between us and them.

John - I'd hate to ask Zoc again to send another dispatch.

Heidi - I'll ask him.

John - Please, honey, don't. Zoc's done enough for us already.

Heidi - If I could hint a little, maybe he'd take the bait and...

John - You're on your own now Heidi. Do what you have to.

Heidi - Thanks, honey.

John - Shakes his head, raises brows.

Heidi - I'm going to tell Connie and Tom...see what they think.

John - Be my guest.

(A short while later).

Heidi - John, Connie and Tom are curious about Paul and Lucy too.

John - So you're going to hint or ask Zoc?

Heidi - Best way to come right out and ask, can't hurt.

John - Remember Zoc's pretty busy running things!

Heidi - I'll wait till he sees us. Then if he's not busy I'll ask.

The time came when the ship was celebrating one of their Anforian holidays. Half the crew were there while the other half maintained the ship. After they would change over. On the second half is when Zoc appears. (This was Heidi's chance to ask)

Heidi - Happy holiday, Zoc.

Zoc - Well thank you Heidi, enjoying yourself?

Heidi - Most definitely. It's too bad Paul and Lucy aren't here.

Zoc - Okay, Heidi, what's on your mind?

Heidi - You see right through me!

Zoc - I'm getting better every day that I'm among you four.

Heidi - Then you won't mind me asking for another favor?

Zoc - What is it Heidi?

Heidi - Would you send another message home and find out anything at all about our friends?

Zoc - They are dead by now!

Heidi - I realize this. We're, or I should say, I'm curious of their life on Anfora.

Zoc - Okay, Heidi. I'll send out another message and find out as much as I can.

Heidi - Oh, thank you Zoc.

Zoc - It won't take as long for an answer this time.

We're a lot closer now. We should get a reply within say two weeks at most.

After the holidays were over Zoc asked Babe to send another message. Give me as much information as possible concerning Professor Paul Burrows and wife, Lucy. Only respond to what happened after Professor Burrows was released. Send reply ASAP. Zoc Less than two weeks later Zoc receives his reply.

To Commander Zoc
From Space Center, Anfora

Professor Burrows retained his position in the Anfora Chemical Plant. Two years later he came up with a chemical process which made him famous and wealthy. Promoted to Head Chemist. One year later Lucy Burrows dies; chronic heart failure, age thirty-four years old. Professor Paul Burrows never remarried and died in his sleep. He was seventy-six years old.

Headquarters Anfora Space Center

Signed Ludi Materazo

Zoc returns to the groups cabins and informs them of the message received.

Heidi - Oh, poor Lucy, so young.

Connie - Lucy always had a heart condition.

Heidi - I didn't know that!

Connie - She told me back in high school and told me not to say anything to anyone.

Tom - Boy, thirty-four years old. Way too young to die.

John - Paul must have known of her condition. still it must have come as a shock.

Tom - One thing we all agree on is that Paul was a real smart man. Too bad we weren't there for him.

Heidi - Thanks, Zoc, for telling us. We do appreciate it,

Zoc - You knew they were dead. Yet none of us realized your friend Lucy had died so young. I'm very sorry.

All members were back to duty now. The girls were free to do whatever they wanted. They decided to keep working, at what, they didn't know. But something... they were eventually assigned to the (galley) kitchen. As for the boys, they took over the maintenance of the computer. They were responsible as if they were part of the crew; upholding the admiration of the other crewmen and Zoc, of course.

Time seemed to go by faster now and the ship would be getting ever so much closer to Anfora. It wouldn't be long new until touchdown on Anfora again after so long a time. The four seemed to be a little edgy as they got closer and closer to their final, if not their last stop. Zoc could sense the apprehansion among them, but didn't try to approach or try to calm their fears. Zoc realized their fears. He had told them many times before... but alas it didn't seem to penetrate. Zoc knew precisely when they would arrive, waiting to see if one or more would ask... they never did. Maybe not knowing was better all around.

The waiting was just about over for the four. Anfora was in sight and it would only be weeks now till they landed.

Two weeks before they were to land the small group of four assembled in one of their cabins, knelt to pray, asking for a just and fair trial, and asked God to forgive them.

Approaching runway, secure, prepare for landing. The girls were in the kitchen. The boys were on the Bridge with Zoc.

Zoc - Ease up, you two, it's almost over. Relax. Touchdown...

The ship comes to a halt. The ramp extended and all but a few disembark. Sibi escorts the girls up to Zoc. Zoc, Sibi and the group are last to leave the ship.

Waiting at the ramp of the craft was a deputy of the court.

Deputy - Which one of you is Commander Zoc?

Zoc - I am, came the reply.

Deputy - Received your wire sir. The Commissioner has honored your request and has accepted the bond.

You will be contacted in four to six weeks. Good night, Sir.

Zoc - Good night.

Just then a car approaches the craft. A courier jumps out. Are you Commander Zoc?

Zoc - Yes?

Courier - I have a sealed letter here from Paul Burrows to Mr. Mon'e or John Hodges.

Zoc - Thank you. Passes the letter to John.

John reads the letter aloud.

Dear Space Travelers:

I pray every day that you made it home. If you did then I've written this for nothing. In the event you were captured and brought back to Anfora, this letter is meant for you. On your arrival you will be met by my legal attorneys. They will represent all of you. All legal fees will be taken out of my estate. Don't worry. I've made a small fortune here on Anfora. Lucy and I have no heirs so the money you may need is all yours.

Best of Luck Professor Paul and Lucy

Zoc - Bring a car around.

Sibi - Yes, Sir.

(Leaves)

John - You put up a bond for us so we wouldn't spend the time in jail till the trial! You're something else Zoc!

(Car arrives)

Okay, pile in. We're headed for the apartment.

(At the apartment)

Zoc - Tomorrow with the lawyers; they can go over your defense. Just remember one thing...You did not steal the space craft...you only borrowed it! Do you understand?

All - Yes, Zoc.

Zoc - I'll see you all tomorrow afternoon. Sibi and I have some things to attend to. One more thing. Get in touch with Paul Burrows' attorneys as soon as possible. Good night.

All - Goodnight Zoc, thanks ever so much. The next morning Tom calls the Burrows attorneys to let them know that they received the letter and needed their help.

Tom - Their sending over two attorneys in about an hour.

John - I was just wondering what Zoc has on his mind?

Tom - I'm curious myself. Whatever is up his sleeve we'll know soon enough.

Connie - Whatever it is, I'm sure Zoc can fix it.

Tom - I hope so.

John - You've been very quiet since we've landed. Anything wrong?

Heidi - I'm terrified, I keep thinking of life in a jail cell.

John - I'm almost positive you two girls will get no more than a slap on the wrist.

Heidi - I'm worried about all of us, not just myself.

John - I realize your concern. Just look at what happened to Paul. Just a fine...nothing more.

Heidi - I just wish I were as confident as you two are.

Tom - Look, Heidi. John's right, we have lots of help new, plus money we didn't count on. According to the late Burrows' estate, he was a billionaire.

Heidi - Money can't buy everything, Tom.

Just then the doorbell rings.

Connie answers the door.

Good morning. We're looking for Mr. and Mrs. Mon'e and Mr. and Mrs. Hodges. We're from the late Professor's estate.

Connie - Yes, of course. Come in. We've been expecting you.

All eight sat down at the table.

Each one tells the attorneys what had preceeded and the attorneys told them what to say or leave out of their testimonies, unless specific questions were asked. The attorneys questioned them one by one.

Tom - Now you're badgering us!

One attorney - Of course, what do you think the opposition is going to do?

Tom - Point well taken.

Zoc finally arrives along with Sibi. They join the group. Question after question is asked. Late afternoon came and they were still at it.

Heidi - Can we break for now and get something to eat.

All agree to call it a day and continue tomorrow. The attorneys left. Zoc stayed behind to have dinner with them, Sibi included. After dinner Zoc said things look very good as far as he could tell, but it was still up to the court to decide.

The following day rehearsal of the upcoming trial would commence again.

# Chapter 12

## *The Trial*

The time had come. They had braved many things, but this was different.

The car had arrived to take them to their unknown destiny. Once in the car no one spoke. They looked at each other and out the windows of the car. It had snowed the night before. Now a freezing rain was falling. The car rolled forward at a steady pace. It seemed like a slow motion dream to the four accused. The car soon came to a halt outside a huge hangar at the Space Center. Was this the place for the trial? They were led out. Walking through the mixture of snow and freezing rain, the sky was dark as were their spirits.

John and Tom both worried for their wives, praying that the girls would be acquitted.

They enter the hangar; it was enormous, but empty except for two tables and the rows of folding chairs facing the benches.

Once seated Zoc leans over and whispers I believe their only trying to intimidate you. Tom - It's working!

Zoc - Relax.

In the second row sat the attorneys with Sibi and Tolo. First to arrive was the court appointed stenographer followed by six judges. All rose and then were told to be seated.

1st Judge - Are the accused present?

Yes, your Honor, came the reply.

Are the accused represented by counsel?

Again came the yes answer.

1st Judge - Then let us begin. As I call your names you will stand and swear to the testimony you are about to give.

First - John Hodges swears

Second - Thomas Mon'e swears

Third - Heidi Hodges swears

Fourth - Connie Mon'e swears

1st Judge - You can all be seated. One by one they were questioned by the prosecution and the defending attorneys.

All through the trial there were many objections, some sustained, others permitted. The five days' ordeal was starting to show on the four.

On the sixth day the prosecution rested their case followed by the defense attorneys.

The judges rose and left the hangar to go over the case and render a verdict.

For two days the judges went over the transcript. Finally they came back. All were assembled.

1st Judge - On hearing both sides of this case we are still left with several questions that puzzle us.

Zoc - May I approach the bench?

1st Judge - Yes, Commander Zoc, if you could clarify some of the mystery.

Zoc - I think I can, your Honor.

1st Judge - One...How did you get to Earth before they did?

You left two days after they left.

Zoc - Pure chance. I'm a trained navigator and way better than the accused.

1st Judge - Hum! Well you stated they didn't steal the space craft; that they only borrowed it?

Zoc - Yes, your Honor.

1st Judge - How can you prove this?

Zoc - I had my second-in-command, Lt. Sibi get a recording from the computer.

1st Judge - Inadmissable!

Zoc - Your Honor, please, a computer doesn't lie. It can only execute orders fed into it.

1st Judge - Okay, proceed.

Zoc - Motions to Sibi. Bring the recorder tape. (plays tape).

John's voice on tape. Okay Babe on my signal beam us down.

Clicks off. This proves that the craft was not stolen, but borrowed. Otherwise they would have landed the craft on Earth.

1st Judge - What makes you sure the craft wouldn't be taken afterward by other earthlings?

Zoc - It was programmed to return to Anfora. The computer will also verify this.

1st Judge - I'll take your word on that. But whether stolen or borrowed it is still a felony!

Zoc - Your Honor, their only crime I see is the want of their home world.

1st Judge - I see, but you don't see. I'm the Judge, not you, am I clear?

Zoc - Yes, your Honor. May I speak of the help the earthlings offered me as well as the Anfora Government?

1st Judge - Proceed.

Zoc - Testimony was given of the borrowing of the ship and the capture and return. Nothing else was mentioned of what happened on our way back.

1st Judge - If it's about the new planet, the court knows of this already. It's in all the papers.

Zoc - Well, your Honor, that's only part of it. The gamma ray burst may have helped us find the planet. But if we didn't go after the earthlings none of this would have happened.

1st Judge - You're forgetting two lost crewmen and several injured.

Zoc - No, I'm not forgetting them at all. But if it wasn't for Tom and John, the whole crew would be missing if not for their help.

1st Judge - Irrelevent. If it wasn't for those two none of this would have occurred at all.

Zoc - But it did! Look at it this way. We discovered a new world! Think of what that means to the wealth of our Nation.

1st Judge - That part is true. I would like to ask you a personal question Zoc. You were the escape goat from the beginning, yet you choose to defend them?

Zoc - I've gotten to know them personally, each one, unique. Plus this all happened before you were born your Honor. Two hundred plus years is a long time to hold a grudge by the Anfora people.

1st Judge - One thing I will tell you. We did arrive at a verdict of the two women Heidi and Connie and that was to let them go! No charges will be filed!

Tom and John look at each other, wide smiles and a high five.

1st Judge - We will go back with this new information and give you our findings. Court dismissed.

They all leave. John and Tom are ecstatic. Their prayers were answered. The day seemed much brighter now than it was when they first started out.

Heidi - How can you two be so happy. Everything is still up in the air about your fate.

John - We're happy for you two!

Tom - And don't worry about us; we'll survive!

Connie - If anything happens to you two then our freedom means nothing.

Zoc - I'm happy for you too girls and don't fret about your husbands. I'm sure it will all turn in their favor.

Heidi - I sure wish we had your outlook.

Zoc - Right now return home. Get some rest and take your minds off all of this. Please!

Tom - You're right Zoc, no sense working up a sweat if you can't predict the future.

(The following morning).

Zoc and Sibi arrive to get the group and return to the hangar and hear the verdict. Both girls were fearing the outcome not being in the boys' favor.

Once inside John and Tom would face the six judges and listen to the verdict.

Mr. Hodges and Mr. Mon'e you have been found guilty of the crime presented to this court.

(Both girls gasp)

Do you have anything to say before the veridct is handed down? John and Tom look at each other, then nod to each other. No, your Honor.

Then the court will pass sentence. Both of you will be fined five thousand dollars a piece and will be sent to the (Tom and John thinks, here it comes, jail time) new planet where you will remain. Court dismissed.

Zoc - Congratulations. You won! A small fine and extradited to the new world.

The girls are kissing their husbands. Thank God there was no jail time.

John - I'm glad it turned out as it did. No jail time, a small fine that we can well afford. Just one thing worries me. We're not pioneers. We're city folks. We won't last two weeks in the wild country!

Zoc - Do you think that you four are the only people going to the planet...think again.

Tom - Maybe not, but John's right. We're not pioneers and we won't last.

Zoc - I have news for all of you. In the newspapers and on the helostation (television); of course you couldn't possibly know this. Anfora's planning a large migration to the new world. It's all in Anfora's language. Therefore you couldn't know, but new space crafts are being built right now as we speak. Thousands have signed on. Miners, engineers, biologists, chemists, etc., plus homesteaders. Roads will be paved, buildings erected. It is said that within two years it will be a second Anfora! With the money Paul Burrows left you, you could build a dream house of your choice. Don't forget you can hire anyone you want to build your future. Now what, pioneers?

Heidi - Zoc's right. This is a great opportunity.

Tom - I wonder what the price of reality will be?

Zoc - My guess. Stake out a claim, say a thousand acres a piece before prices are set. According to some reports ten ships have already departed for the new world.

John - Since some crafts have already left, when do we go?

Zoc - The Judge never specified a set time for your departure.

John - Then we have time to plan!

Zoc - Make your plan fast as he (the Judge) may realize he never set a date!

Tom - Is it possible to get a detailed plan of the new world site?

Zoc - That's a good idea. I'm sure they have one. If so, I'll obtain a copy. I'll leave now and get back to you later.

(Later that day)

John - Tom, I've come up with a plan!

Tom - Not another Plan "A" - Plan "B"?

John - No! Not like that. A preparation plan.

Tom - Okay, I'm listening.

John - When Zoc returns with the layout of the city.

Tom - If there is one!

John - We can plan our homes close to the city.

Tom - So?

John - We have to bring money, second (2nd) obtain a craft for all the things we'll need and store aboard.

Tom - Obtain a craft. I hope you mean charter one?

John - Of course or buy one?

Tom - Even with our money I'm sure we couldn't afford that!

John - Okay, scratch one purchase. Besides we'll need money for other things.

Tom - We're free, but not to the extent of running around purchasing things.

John - So we'll get some one else to purchase for us.

I'll check with Zoc to be sure.

(The following morning)

Zoc arrives with the plans for the new city.

Zoc - One other thing I found out for you. Acreage is going at twenty-five dollars an acre. My suggestion is to pay before you go, otherwise you may only be able to purchase acreage too far away from the city.

Tom - I'll get the Burrows lawyers to purchase the acreage forms.

John - Since our conviction is it possible to buy land?

Zoc - Of course!

John - We plan to rent a space craft.

Zoc - No need to. The judges are sending you. No charge.

John - But we wanted to bring many things with us. We need room.

Zoc - These new ccraft are twice as large as the old ones.

The old craft held three hundred crewmen plus food, water - observation deck, hospital - rec room and dining halls, etc., etc. Three elevators, numerous stairwells, decks - shall I go on?

Tom - I almost forgot how big it was.

Zoc - Purchase what you need. Have it crated, marked and shipped to this address. (Zoc jots down address).

John - I wish you would be our Commander on our flight to the new world.

Zoc - But I will be. I was already told, but not when.

Tom - Great news.

Zoc - Start as if you were going yesterday! Sibi is at your disposal. Time is running out.

Tom sends a courier to the (Burrows) attorneys with the proposed acreage marked off in red on the enclosed map of the new world. Plus X amount of cash to be delivered to the Zoc apartment.

John/Tom had hired a couple dozen men to purchase the equipment they will need and ship it to the address Zoc had written down. Carpenters were standing by to crate items and itemize its contents on the outside of the crates.

Not crated were two four-wheel-drive gas autos.

Tom - Did we forget anything?

John - It's possible, but I don't think we did.

Tom - I'll contact Zoc.

Hello Zoc? Tom here.

Zoc - Hello Tom, all set?

Tom - Yes, everything is crated and ready for pickup.

Zoc - Good! I'll have it picked up and shipped to the Space Center.

Tom - When will it be loaded aboard the craft?

Zoc - As soon as I'm assigned a new space craft it will be stowed away.

Tom - Do you have any idea when that'll be?

Zoc - Soon now I'm sure. Just go over your list and make sure you have everything you might need. Once we leave there's no going back!

Tom - In any event we do miss something we would send for it, no?

Zoc - No! Distance to the new planet is too far away. By the time you'd receive it, you'd be too old to need it.

Tom laughs...you're right, there's no overnight deliveries!

Zoc - I'll get your stuff over to the Space Center and like I said, if there is more things you need, ship them directly to the Space Center "Marked for Commander Zoc".

Tom - Thanks a million, Zoc! Bye.

Two weeks later

John - Hey, gang, tomorrow Sibis picking us up.

Heidi - Well this is it!

Connie - Worried Heidi?

Heidi - (apprehensivly) - Maybe!

Tom - We forgot one thing!

John - What?

Tom - To withdraw our money out of the bank and have it transfered!

John - Then do it quick!

Tom - I'm on it.

Moments later.

Tom - OK, money will be transfered to the new bank as soon as they receive notice as to where that might be.

John - We'd better contact Zoc again.

Tom - Your turn, buddy.

John calls Zoc.

Tom - Well John?

Zoc says not to worry, get vouchers from the bank, just as good as money.

John calls again, gets a balance of the account and asks to have it sent to them in vouchers ASAP, We are leaving tomorrow.

Connie - I hope we're all ready to go now

Tom - Is there anything else John ?

John - I believe we have everything.

Heidi - This time tomorrow we'll be on our way to our new home.

Connie - The only thing Heidi and I saw was through a porthole, what's it like on this new planet guys ?

Tom - Lush valleys clear water and plenty of fresh air.

John - A beautiful world no question about it.

Tom - Also we won't be pioneers or be alone.

John - Let's pray that this is our final and last trek.

(Courier at door)

Mr MON'E or MR.HODGES telegram.

Yes came the reply, come in.

I'm from the exchange,I have your vochers.

Tom - Thank you.

Courier - Sign here and here. Tom signs.

Courier - need your signiture too. John signs

Thank you very much.John then hands the courier a sizable tip.

Courier - Thank you very much gentlemen. Courier leaves.

John - Now we sit back and wait for Sibi!

Tom - How much money do we have left ?

John opens the envelope, Hmm many denominations and the invoice a total amount!

Tom - Well John?

John - would you believe wer'e still billionairs!

Tom - After- all we spent!

John - It would appear so,see for yourself.

Tom - Looks as though we only spent a small portion of the interest. Whoa!

Sibi knocks Come in sibi,come in.

Sibi - Are we ready to go?

John- Its now or never', wer'e ready!

At the space center Sibi points out their craft.

Heidi- It's enormous!

Connie - Not round like the old one.

Sibi - Completely changed from top to bottom!

Heidi - Very stylish Sibi!

Sibi - Stylish? It's not a new dress I

John - Heidi means it's more stream lined!

Sibi - Ah yes. I see, Shall we board?

( After entering the craft)

Sibi - says let me show you the interior. One of the surprises was their new quarters, twice as large as the old one. It was located mid ship, Everything was bigger and better,one could get lost in such a craft. On each deck posted signs showed where you were and how to get to any part of this giantic ship.

Sibi - we'll be tacking off soon, looks at his watch less than two hours I'd say. Make yourselves comfortable, I'll see you after we take off.

Time seemed to inch by ever-so-slowly

( Over the intercom ) Prepare for lift off. Well gang here we go, says Tom.

The big craft lifted off the pad and headed out, they were on their way

John - Look we're over anfora, It doesn't seem as though wer'e moving!

Connie - Like sleeping on a cloud.

Intercom you may remove your saftey belts. Just then a knock at the door.

John - That'll be Sibi!

To John's surprise it was Zoc,not Sibi.

Zoc - You where expecting Sibi ?

John - As amatter of fact we wer'e.

Zoc - I didn't get to talk to all of you before we left.

Tom - We understand,A commander has plenty to do.

Zoc - All your things are secured, And you have your vouchers?

Tom - Yes, everything seems to be in order.

Zoc- As you know this flight is just under twenty five light years away.

John - I'm puzzled ,Earth is one hundred light years away, and this new planet is only twenty light years away how is it possible not to have discovered it before?

Zoc - I wondered about that myself, odd isn't it!

John - Most odd indeed!

*Anfora*

Zoc - To change the subject for a moment,I have a surprise for you!

Tom - And ?

Zoc - The new computer that was installed has some of Babes memory banks installed with the new and faster computer!

John - Hey that's great! I gather you still call her babe?

Zoc - Of course,I wouldn't have it any other way!

John - When can we come to the bridge and talk to Babe?

Zoc - Yes! just as before.

Heidi - Will you be staying with us on the new planet?

Zoc - Only long enough to unload the cargo and make sure it gets to the right location.Then back to Anfora for my next assignmet.

Heidi - When will you return?

Zoc - I never know when or where they'll send me next.

Heidi - Oh Zoc! We may never see you again.

Zoc - A round trip would take Fifty light years and if I did , you'd be to old to recognize me! Laughts.

Connie - However long it may be we'd never forget you!

Zoc - I'm flattered.

John - Why not give up your command and settle down!

Zoc - I get itchy feet, I am and always will be an explorer nothing more nothing less!

John - One of the things we purchased was a two way radio to keep in touch with you in the event you wouldn't stay.

Zoc - You boys are always thinking of something.

Tom - You've done so much for us that we feel your part of the family, why not keep in touch?

Zoc - Wer'e all humans on earth like you four?

John - God forbid! The world is better off without us!

Zoc - I doubt that.

Heidi - Please have dinner with us tonight?

Zoc - DON'T YOU THINK I HAVE BETTER THINGS TO DO!!

All - Brows raised - What?

Zoc - gotcha! Yes of course, laughs.

Connie - I swear Zoc your getting more humanized everyday!

Zoc - So what time?

Heidi - It's up to you.

Zoc - Sibi can stay at the helm for the rest of the day, hows six tonight?

Heidi - Well then six it is.

Zoc - have to run now, see you: at six.

Zoc leaves Heidi - It seems Zoc's picked up some humor!

John - Zoc has many facets to his name its all good.

( weeks roll by, then months ) How close where they ?

They asked Zoc.

Zoc told them to ask babe.

John - Babe how long will it be to reach the new planet?

Babe - at the current rate we will arrive in three weeks,fourteen hours and forty two seconds, John.

John - You recognized my voice!

Babe - Of course! You gave me my name remember?

John - Nice talking to you again Babe!

Babe - Nice hearing you again John.

John - Zoc that's unbelieveable.

Zoc - Babe has the ability to correct you if your wrong.

Landing right on time to the second as Babe had said.

Beneath them stood the city almost complete, construction, was everywhere.So many people as Zoc had said. Most streets and highways where completed or underconstruction.

All Disembarked Lt. Tolo supervised the unloading, serparating the cargo. Zoc had Sibi assigned to take the crates and other materials off and separate each item ,making sure that each would get to it's proper location.

Trucks came in loaded up and sent out.

Except for crates,Zoc would deliever this load personally. It took most of the morning, after the trucks where loaded.

John and Heidi along with Tom and Connie followed in their new cars behind Tolo and Sibi. Arriving at their new homes.

Sibi - Here we are.

Connie I can't believe the houses are built already!

Sibi - According to your specks too. Don't forget the time frame, It took years to build your homes.

John - Sibi we need workmen to help us uncrate all this!

Sibi - Way ahead of you, Zoc is at the present time selecting a crew for you, He should be along any time

John - Sibi those two crates over there marked hardware should have been left in town.

Sibi - Why so !

John - For our new hardware store Tom and myself are opening. This new area will need hardware supplies.

( Moments later )

Connie - Look there's Zoc with a truck load of men.

Sibi - That's your work crew!

John - Zoc am I glad to see you.

Zoc - Well let's get started and unload. I have one man here who speaks english, he can be of great value to you.

John - thanks Zoc.

Zoc - My pleasure.

By mid after noon all the furniture was set up in both houses, both girls gave Zoc, Sibi and Tolo a tour of the houses, John and Tom had helped the crew and said thanks for their help. The worker who spoke English was to stay behind and assist with jobs needed around the place. Later he was hired full time to help at the hardware store, his name was Therm.

John - How much time do you have before you return to Anfora ?

Zoc - I was given two weeks to complete my mission here then back home again.

John - Two weeks that's not much time to spend with us.

Connie - Why not come to dinner at our house, along with Tolo and Sibi?

ZOC Well men, what do you say,dinner!

Both Sibi and Tolo whole heartely agreed.

Dinner was set for the following evening.

That evening the food was brought in, a banquet fit for a king.

Zoc was impressed as well as Sibi and Tolo.

Zoc - Sibi tells me your opening a hardware store down town.

Tom - that we are Zoc the town will need one.

Sibi - that's what the two crates are for,we'll take them down to town tomorrow.

After all they had been through, they at last settled down to their new way of life. The world they left behind was now just a memory, But not totally forgotten. At times they would reminisce.

For the most part they where busy with the present.

Zoc had since left with Sibi and Tolo. The group had made some new friends through the summer, Fall was soon approaching. Therm was now manager of the hardware store and the store was doing a booming business. The girls had hire hired a small staff to help around the homes. They wer'e happy They where happy. But something was missing.

The girls talked, was it time to start a family?

Would tom and John agree? Was it to soon?

Would they want a family so soon after being here for less than a year? They had everything that money could buy! so why not ask.

Tom and John where starting to learn the Anforian language, slowly at first and gradually picking up more and more.They knew it would be some time before they could the language fluently. The girls on the other hand never tried to learn the language, why bother the servants spoke English.

# Chapter 13

## *The UNKNOWN*

The hardware store was doing better than expected.

They had more money then they needed, both decided to give most of the proceeds to local charity

Living off the interest was more money to live on for the rest of their lives! The girls where pleased with this decission. The boys would go to work everyday and the girls would stay home and take care of their daily jobs. At the hardware store business was so good, that it wouldn't take very long before the stock could run out. What was to be done, Even if they radioed ahead, it still would be some twenty five light years away. Tom had estimated the stock would be depleted in about two years!

Back on ANFORIA

At the Observatory Atho was scanning the sky around the new planet, when he discovered something unusual, hey Pai look at this!

Pai peeps through the telescope, what! I don't see Anything....

Atho - Look again, notice anything out of the ordinary?

Get me the photo plate from yesterday, then you'll see.

Pai gets the plate taken the previous night. He and Atho then compare them. There was definitely a difference between the two. Slight but never the less a change.

Atho - We need older plates to compare with these!

Pai - I'll check to see if we have any!

Atho - Any luck?

Pai - The oldest one we have is only eight months old, nothing else.

Atho - Let's take a look.

Pai - The planet is even farther away from where it was eight months ago.

Atho -Let's contact other Observatories and find out if they have any plates older then we have, the older the better.

Sure enough they had and would send them over.

Pai - Now we wait.

Two days later they arrived.

Atho - Ready Pai?

Pai - Yes, let's compare.

Comparing the oldest plate with the new one proved without any doubt that the planet was not seen on the plate! I appeared to have come out of nowhere!

So far the new planet is keeping it's orbit around the star, but it but seems a little erractic.

Right now all we can do is observe.

Pai - We'll have to take more and more pictures comparing again and again before we make our final report.

Atho - Then we'd better get started.

Pai - The sooner the better!

For four months, every night, seven days a week Atho and Pai took scores of photographic plates of the region.

The new planet was here now but not before. It was confirmed by other Observatories. Make no mistake, it was there. But where did it come from!

Speculation abound in the astronomy field! Was there any explanation? The news papers called the new planet THE ENIGMA PLANET!

All Astronomers studied the plates. There had to be an answer, But what!

While Atho and Pai studied more of the surrounding region they both discovered something that they and others had missed, A rift in space. Could this planet have come through? Another dimension? There was a distortion in and around where they first photographed the new planet! Could this be the answer? Telling the other Observatories of their finding and see what they would come up with.

Other astronomers agreed with Pai and Atho's findings

Also they concluded that the rift was getting larger, which was causing the planets erratic orbit.

How much larger the rift was going to get was anyones guess. At the present rate of expansion the planet was sure to rip itself apart!

The government had to be notified immediately of the impending danger that faced the people.

How much time was left before this would occur couldn't be determed with the lack of data at hand, But it will occur!

The government contacted the space center, telling them of the Observatories findings.

The space center took it from there. Contacting all craft enroute home, return back and unload all cargo, all craft on said planet stay there and unload all your cargo also, all craft will be boarding passengers, New planet in peril!

The new planet

The message reached the new planet,The group heard it from Therm.

Heidi - Every time we get set or plan anything,something always goes wrong!

Connie - You can say that again, WE can't win!

The craft that was there started to unload their cargo. Other craft that had left including Zoc's turn around and headed back to the new planet. Many craft had to remain in orbit, waiting their turn to land.It was sugested to move south to a better location, So more craft could land and start unloading faster, also also an alphabetical arrangement was imposed, Last names starting with "A" through "N" would stay North and "M" through "Z" would proceed South. This would help alleveate some of the back up.

When John and Heidi heard of the new arrangement they traded places with Therm and his wife. The group had stayed together through thick and thin, John and Heid won't be separated from their friends. They would head South with Tom and Connie!

Tom - Don't be foolish you two,don't wait for us it may be your only way out. board the craft asigned to you!

Heidi - AS John says ....we came together we go together, we're a team!

Connie - You two are making a big mistake. What happens if we don't make it? Then What?

Heidi - We've lived together, we die together!

Tom - I guess they come south with us.

Heidi - Good that's all set!

In just two days five more craft had landed and been unloaded, Now personel where begining to board the ships. At eight hundred souls per crafty four thousand where now heading back to ANFORA!

Counting the total space craft to date , It would bring the total up to three thousand personel so far. The convoys where ready and loaded with provisions and fuel for the trucks and vehicles, started their trek south, not to far, just over a hundred fifty miles.

It was now that the group filed in behind each other in single file. Every third or forth truck was followed by many vechicles.

Thirty thousand people remained north,while the other Thirty Three thousand headed south.

Each morning the sun would appear in a different section of sky, most didn't notice, not many of them: did. Slight tremors and where becoming more violent as days rolled on. Rumble was heard now and then as they pressed on south, no paved roads this far south made the going worse, the farther they went. A small earth quake opened the ground, trees fell,and rocks had to be removed before continuing on. Driving became very harzardous, many vehicles broke down, everyone was sore and tired.

Back on ANFORA

Pai - heres another plate Atho,the rift has gotten bigger much bigger since last night.

Atho - At this rate the planet doesn't seem to have much time left,before she rips herself apart! Pai - It's up another four per cent.

Atho - I'm wondering how much time those people have, before all hell breaks out!

Pai - judging by our findings, The rate of wobble has increased three fold,in less then a week.

If this continues at its present pace, The planet will bolw before anyone can be evacuated!

Atho - I'm calling the space center and giving them our latest data, But I can't see them doing anything, That their not already doing!

Pai - That'll shake them up, Maybe they'll move a little faster.

Atho - I'm sure their doing all that is possible!

Pai - What do you think of their chances?

Atho - If they can send enough ships ( within range ) it's a good chance for a full evacuation.

Pai - I'd hate to be in their shoes!

Atho - Be thankful your here on ANFORA! not there.

Pai - I PRAY they make it!

Atho - Yes, But they need time, precious time.

Back at the planet

Tremors where felt althrough the night, Many couldn't sleep. Those who did where restless.

To those who took notice, The sun came up some six, or more degrees off in the past twelve hours than in the past few days.

More tremors followed by more and bigger quakes.

No one there could measure them, But some estimated it was between six and seven.

John - we've all been through so much and just when we think our ship has come in, We get involved with some - thing else.

Connie - John you sound like an echol

John - How so?

Connie - Heidi said basicly the same thing a few days ago.

John - Two minds with a single though!

Tom - That's life John,Little ups and downs.

Heidi - WE may not be able to predict the future, But i'm an optimist, We'll endure.

John - Your just what the doctor ordered.

Sweetheart! We've lost our world we lost our home we lost our business, But not each other, I'm proud of you Heidi. Heidi kisses John.

Heidi - You know I'll miss our new house here,little America!

John - when did you start calling our home little America?

Heidi - Right after we moved in,Connie knew.

John - Your a romantic Heidi.

Heidi do you want to trade me in?

John - Laughs, I'd loved you from the first time I saw you and through eternity I will still love you.

I wouldn't trade you in for anyone or anything, In this world or the next!

Heidi - John your such a romantic yourself.

Tom - have you two deceided what you'll do if we make it out of here.

John - Heidi and I haven't discussed it yet. same as you and Connie will do. Start over again!

Tom - Well we both have lots of money, We could take some time off! Travel, Something new for a change of pace. I don't think Connie and myself want to settle down right away.

Connie - WE need a break from all this,we're tired.

Heidi - John and I hadn't made any plans for our future, We've been to busy and worried about this mess we're in we've had no time to think .

John - Theres plenty of time if we make it to ANFORA!

Tom - If for some reason or another we should have to Leave ANFORA once we get there, Connie would be home sick again. Big smirk.

Connie - Jabs Tom very funny, Very funny indeed! ( they laugh ).

Tom - I'd prefer you'd be home sick for me!

Connie - Wide smile, That goes without saying LOVE That night they helped others unload one of the Craft.

The following morning, Who should appear, It was Zoc!

Tom - Look gang, It's Zoc!

The girls scream with delight,Over here Zoc over here. Waving frantically.

Zoc - Well gang we meet again.

Whatever are you doing here Zoc, You left weeks ago?

I was ordered back to help evacuate all personel ( that includes you four ): I didn't think I'd see you again.

Tom - Now your stuck with us for the duration,And we may not get off this planet.

Zoc - We'll get out okay,One thing I noticed on Lhe roster was that John and Heidi switched places with Therm and his wife to be with you two I knew you'd stick together!

Now I can get you all back to ANFORA....

Together,with me.

Heidi - But Zoc you'll be risking your life to save us.

Zoc - Don't fret about me, Young Lady I'll be fine

Connie - But we do worry about you. You've done so much for us already!

Zoc - To change the subject...(Stating firmly) GET ME SOMETHING TO EAT, AND I MEAN RIGHT NOW AND MOVE IT PRONTO. DO YOU READ ME?

They all looked at each other in amazement! What? Then Zoc burst out laughing....GOTCHA! again more and more laughter.

Tom - You had us going there for a minute.

Zoc - Remember ...What's up doc! ..Now we're even.

Tom - Sure! But you didn't know what Heidi was referring to!

Zoc - Not then, But later I found out .

Connie - Your getting to be like an earthling every day!

Zoc - Lets not go over board, No intent meant. Now they all laughed.

John - I'm glad your here under any circumstances.

Zoc - Glad to oblige.

Although conditions worsened by the day, all anforians and the group managed to sustain only minor injuries.

At the rate of evacuation and the rate of earth quakes, it would surely escalate. Zoc had figured at the onset at least forty craft to evacuate everyone. Four a week.

To be on the safe side. Eight or more where needed twice a week to keep up with the conditions facing them.

At the Anfora observatory the rift was getting bigger, much bigger! The planets orbit was well over fourteen percent (14%) They contacted the space center of their findings.

John - Zoc how is it possible to get here before this planet destroys us. Where twenty five light years from Anfora?

Zoc - The ship including mine had just left here for Anfora and was informed of the situation, we immediatly returned and there you are!

Tom - That explains some things, but not all. We can't survive a twentyfive light year wait from Anfora!

Zoc - My crew and three other craft where the closes to return, but other ships ranging from fifty or more ships, had left here only weeks before me. Therefore they will arrive weeks from now or, sooner.

Tom - Well, that's a relief!

Zoc - Everyone will be evacuated. So many people, so little time! Would they make it? Only time will tell. Earth Quakes were now opening the ground around them. Many cars were overturned, fires started, but soon extinguished. No one dared start a fire to cook meals, meals were served cold. Waiting for the ships was agonizing. When were they coming? The wait was not long in coming. One by one the craft landed. What awaited was the cargo to be unloaded. Squads were chosen to remove the ore etc. and leave the forklifts and equipment behind. Some craft were unloaded faster then others, as each craft finished, the boarding started, one by one they took off. Zoc's ship was almost ready. In the few days nine more craft arrived. The crew of men needed to get everyone off the planet, needed more time as fewer and fewer men were available. Zoc asked his crew to volunteer as did the commander of the last six crafts. Working together, this would expidite matters and be more efficient. Finally all crafts were loaded and ready for departure.

Aboard the craft now was the group. Zoc at the helm. The four settled down.

John - For a while there, I didn't think we'd make it.

Tom - Well buddy, whats our next adventure!

John - Well I have a plan! Pillows start flying all at John. John laughs, I'm only kidding.

All - We know! More pillows.

John - It's so goodl (knock at hatch) Enter, comes the reply.

Zoc - We'll be taking off shortly.

Tom - What are we waiting for?

Zoc - We are going to be the last to leave.

Heidi - Why?

Zoc - I want to be very sure every craft leaves. Once we go, there is no going back.

Heidi - You worry about everyone.

Zoc - I ought to remember the trail, I said we could colonise this place . . . Well, I'm responsable for every living soul who landed here.

Tom - Say no more Zoc, I see your point, (intercom)

Commander Zoc to the bridge.

Zoc - On the way.

Zoc - I'll see you all later.

John - By the way, who's your second in command?

Zoc - Lt. Tolo, See you later.

At the helm, Zoc is observing the take off of each craft.

Thinking to himself it won't be long now. Just as the last craft lifts off a tremendous quake shakes Zoc's craft.

Zoc - Computer begin lift off!

Computer - Yes Commander.

The craft shuddlers as it slowly rises from the ground.

Heidi - What was that?

John - Another quake!

Tom - Here we go again!

John - No! We are gaining altitude

Tom - We are airborne, yahoo!

John - Go for it Zoc!

Connie - Are we ok!

Tom - I think so.

John unbuckles and goes to the portal.

Tom - Hey John, get back in your seat and buckle up.

John - Right, I was just checking.

(intercom) This is Commander Zoc, We are safly above the planet now. The planet was giving us a final goodbye with a major earth quake.

(moments later) A rap at the hatch. Enter.

Tom - Zoc glad your back so soon.

Zoc - A little alarmed there were you?

Tom - For a brief second.

Zoc - How would you and John like to join me on the bridge?

Tom - Sounds like old times, you bet we'll be there.

Zoc - Be on the bridge as soon as possible.

Tom - See you later then.

Zoc had no longer left the cabin when the planet exploded.

It rocked the ship. Zoc was thrown across the passage way.

Slowly regaining his footing, raced as fast as he could.

Being knocked from one side to the other, he managed to reach the elevator.

Tom - Holy Shit what was that?

John - We'd better see if Zoc 's o'kay. Stay here girls, stay buckled up. Tom and John hedge down the corridor banging from one side to the other. The ship rolled about.

Look, theres Zoc.

John - Are you okay Zoc?

Zoc - I think my ankle is broken.

John - Help me lift Zoc into the elevator.

Zoc - I tried, its not working!

John - Come on lets get Zoc to the infirmary.

Zoc - No bridge!

John - Bridge then it is.

They managed to get Zoc to his feet and some time later they reached the bridge.

Zoc - Lt. Tolo, what's our condition?

Tolo - You hurt sir

Zoc - Never mind, what's our situation?

Tolo - The explosion knocked out a power drive, but we are still intact, no other damage reported.

John - Computer get a doctor to the bridge pronto! Possible broken leg.

Zoc - We don't have time for this.

John - Better make the time. You look whoozy . . . you may pass out.

minutes later..

Tom - Over here Doc, it's Commander Zoc. Sit down Commander let me take a look. Broken we'll need an xray then possibly a cast.

Zoc - Doctor, I can't leave the bridge now, after we are secured. I promise to be down to see you. Just give me something for the pain.

Tolo - Sorry Commander, your health comes first. I'll take command!

Tom - Please listen to Lt Tolo and the doctor. We don't need you passing out.

Zoc - Okay! okayl But Tolo keep me informed at all times, and you Doctor have exactly one half hour, no more. Do you read me.

Doctor - I'll do the best I can.

Zoc - You'll do better then that, now lets get started.

(Tolo takes command)

Tolo - Any power yet?

Computer - No Commander Tolo.

Zoc - How is the situation?

Tolo - Still no power sir.

Zoc - Hold on, how much longer Doctor? Almost finished, I will be there shortly.

Tolo - Okay Commander, we are still being pulled closer to the rift.

Zoc now on crutches, enters onto the bridge.

Zoc - Told I'll take over now.

Tom - Maybe John and I could help the techs?

Zoc - Yes of course. We need to buy time..Go!

Tolo - What happens to us if we enter into the rift Commander?

Zoc - Can't second guess this one. Lets hope we don't have to find out! (intercom)

This is the Commander. Stay buckled until further notified. We are working to regain power at this moment. (intercom)

One half hour later..

This is Commander Zoc, We have not regained power at this time, in less than twelve minutes we will be heading into the rift. What will happen is anyones guess. Take solace in your own way.

Tom - Amen!

Zoc - Tom you and John join your wives, there is nothing more you two can do here Good Luck! Tom - Luck be with us all.

Zoc - Go fast, you both have less than eight minutes! Girls we are back!!

Oh! cries the girls, Quick buckle up we don't have much time left. The guys buckle up and both reach over to kiss and hug their wives maybe for the last time. The girls reach out and take the hands of their husbands and silently pray.

(intercom)

This is Commander Zoc, we have successfully past through the rift with no ill effects. We are now in a different dimension, it appears no different then our own. We are still working on the power system. We are safe for the moment. You may release your seat buckles.

John - How about that, through the rift without feeling a thing, like a hot knife through butter.

Tom - I was sure it was all over for us.

Heidi - But now what?

John - Restore power and head for home.

Tom - Your forgetting one small thing John, we were sucked through the rift nice and easy, but it may not be so easy to return to our own dimension!

Aboard Commander Sibi's craft.

Babe - Commander Sibi

yes Babe what is it.

Babe - Commander Zoc's craft just vanished into the rift

Sibi - Oh my wordl Zoc !!

Zoc!! It can't be!

Babe - I'm afraid its true Commander Sibi.

Sibi - My friends and all those souls lost forever. Lt. take over the bridge. I'm going to my cabin Lt. Yes Commander Sibi

(back aboard Zoc's craft)

Computer - Commander Zoc!

Zoc - Yes

Computer - Engine power back on line, any instructions?

Zoc - Yes, maintain a straight course away from the rift.

Computer - Away?

Zoc - Yes, inform me when when we are three light years away.

Computer - Yes Commander Zoc.

Tolo - Now that we have power back why are we heading away, shouldn't we be heading back through the rift?

Zoc - In time Tolo, in time.

Tolo - You want to explore this new region?

Zoc - No! Tolo shrugs his shoulders. (thinks to himself now whats he up to?)

(at the cabin)

Tom lets go back on the bridge

John - I'm wondering what Zoc's next move is. Coming Girls?

Heidi - You bet.

Hi Zoc says Heidi

Zoc - Well girls, glad you came up.

John - Zoc, boy are you ever born under a lucky star.

Zoc - Hold on John, it's not over yet. I have an idea that may work or it may not. Getting here was easy getting out another.

John - My buddy Tom said the same thing.

Zoc - What I want to do and what the computer can do is two different things.

John - I don't get it?

Zoc - You will when the time comes, rest assured. By the way thanks for your help men.

Tom and John - We are always at your service Zoc.

Zoc - Now if you'd excuse me, I have some calculations to be made.

John - Sure Zoc ... If you need us, we'll be in our cabin.

Tom - Well what do you make of that conversation John?

John - I don't know, but I'm sure Zoc knows what he is doing.

We just have to wait and see.

Connie - Whatever his plan is, I'm sure it will be the right one.

Heidi - I'll go along with that.

Tom - Neither one of you are curious to what Zoc has planned?

Connie - We are just passengers.

Zoc - Well Tolo, I have come up with a plan and I double checked. I.confered with the computer, and with the information at hand. I think its possible.

Tolo - And that being, Sir?

Zoc - Engage twice the speed of light and plow through the rift!

Tolo - Are you crazy?

Zoo - What!

Tolo - With all do respect Sir, twice the speed of light is only a theory, not a fact! Now that we have our normal flight back, we could plow through the rift at light speed!

Zoc - At the speed of light, according to my calculations and confirmed by the computer is not enough speed to pass through the rift.

Tolo - Does the computer believe we could pass through at twice the speed of light!

Zoc - It was confirmed - possitivly

Tolo - Does the computer guarantee we can achieve twice the speed of light?

Zoc - No!

Tolo - But your going to try!

Zoc - Absolutly

Tolo - As second in command, I protest!

Zoc - Duely noted Lt. Tolo

Tolo - So you gamble with all our lives!

Zoc - That will be all Lt Tolo or would you like to be inturned for the rest of this voyage?

Tolo - No Sir!

(intercom)

This is Commander Zoc, we have gone through the rift with no damage or injuries. We now have a chance to head home.

I'm asking each and every one of you to trust my judgement.

The only way home again is back through the rift again, but my calculations show we cannot do it under our present speed! Than we must go to an untried theory.

Twice the speed of light is our only hope. If we don't try, We are stuck in this dimension forever. I will inform everyone when we switch to our new speed.

Tom - Zoc's our last hope. This better work we're out of options...

Connie - Zoc if it doesn't work, can we look for another planet?

Zoc - connie we have over six hundred passengers plus crew, and not enough supplies to go exploring

Heidi - Lets not explore,lets get home. I don't want to starve to death!

John - since twice the speed of light is only a theory it may not work at all, or this ship may fall apart under the strain, then let GOD be with us.

Zoc - Thought about this himself many times in his mind, But there was no other way.

John - I just had a horrible thought, what if the rift closes before we get there?

Tom - Knock it off John, we have enough to worry about!

Heidi- John I never saw you worry about anything, you're always so confident.

John - maybe, but I'm not in control here, we're at the mercy of Zoc.

Heidi - I thought you trusted Zoc!

John - I do, I really do, Just see my position!

Heidi - We all do.

Tom - Johns right he's usually figuring out what to do next.

Connie - he's like a man in hand cuffs.

John - Right on Connie, Thanks, I wish I could control this situation!

Heidi - John please try to relax.

Computer - Commander Zoc,We have reached our destination,Preparing to turn around .

Zoc - Good, give me two minutes before engaging new speed.

Computer - understood Commander Zoc.

The big craft begins its turn and face the rift.

Computer - Commander Zoc, Two minutes till ignition!

You could almost feel the anxiety aboard the entire craft. Very few spoke and everyone seemed wrapped up in their own thoughts.

Trying a new theory not proven was awfully daring and out right, and completely insane! But it was nothing that could be done. Zoc had made up his mind and that was that! Anytime now he would turn and engage the new speed.He was about to become a devil or a saint,Only time would tell! It would take them home or take them to oblivion.

Zoc - thinking to himself (If I could explore this domain, I'd do it, with no second thoughts at all). I have passengers that count on me to get them to safety and home, but it was a pleasant idea! If the rift still exsisted in the future, maybe He could return and explore this new uncharted region. Think of all the wonders never seen before

I'd..............

Computer - Commander Zoc.

Zoc - Yes?

Computer - coming up to your coordinence!

Zoc - At that point make ready to turn, facing the rift and at that moment engage twice the speed of light, When we get through the rift, return to standard once we our away from the pull of the rift.

This is commander Zoc, Prepare yourselves, In two minutes we will be heading back through the rift, Good Luck to all of us!

The time had come to try the unproven theory, this was their last chance, a gamble yes        But their only hope!

Tolo - Commander Zoc are you certain we can do this, We have only a minute left if you want to change your mind.

Zoc - Iv'e every confidence in the ships integrity I'm not sure of the concequences.

Zoc - Computer, after we get through the rift and pass safetly away from the rifts influence, drop down to standard speed.

Computer - Understood Commander Zoc.

Tolo - Thirty seconds to go Commander Zoc.

Zoc - Brace yourself for the ride of your life!

Tolo - Lets hope we can come through this in one piece!

Zoc - Have a little faith in our engineering technology.

Computer - Switch over in ten seconds!

( Zoc to himself five four three two one) ignition

Then the Great ship lounged forward, not what they expected, Was this twice the speed of light?

Zoc - Computer!

Computer - Yes Commander Zoc.

Zoc - What happened! Why are we still in standard speed?

Computer - We're not Commander Zoc we are now traveling at twice the speed of light, as per instructions.

Tolo - looks out the porthole, Commander Zoc, Everything is just a blur...you1ve proven we can exceed twice the speed of light, And with no ill effect.

Zoc - I would have guessed that the change over would render us unconscious, That's why I wanted the computer to switch back to standard speed once we where clear of the rifts influence.

Just in case we blacked out.

Computer - We are back to normal flight pattern Commander Zoc.

ZOC - Thank you, how far are we behind Sibi's craft?

Computer - Three hundred miles, Commander Zoc.

Zoc - Well Tolo we're almost caught up with the fleet!

Tolo - Let me be the first to congradulate you on being the first man to break twice the speed of light. I also want to apologize for doubting you Sir.

Zoc - no apology needed Tolo, none at all and Thank you!

Computer - Commander Zoc, The planet is still there.

Zoc - That's impossible we saw the planet explode!

Tolo - Yes i saw it too!

Zoc - But it's still there!

Tolo - Are you thinking what I'm thinking?

Zoc - I think so, we've gone back in time!!!!

Zoc - computer what is the time when the planet exploded and the present time?

Computer - less than fifteen minutes Commander Zoc!

Zoc - that proves it. We went into the rift and traveled quit a distants before turning and heading back, that there is over one and a half hours alone.

Tolo - Our we now in the present time frame?

Zoc - I beleive so! But let me check with Sibi.

Computer - contact Sibis crafti

Computer- Yes Commander Zoc.

moments later

Zoc - Sibi this is Commander Zoc.

Sibi - Commander your alive ! I saw the planet explode and then your craft enter the rift next thing the planet is back and so are you,I don't understand?

Zoc - We're are many miles behind you, slow down your craft until I get within beaming range,then beam yourself over to my craft I'll then explain it all to you, Zoc out!

When Sibi is within range he beams over to Zoc's craft.

Sibi - It's so good to see you again...I though I'd lost my friend forever! What's going on!

Zoc - Sibi what I'm about to tell you,you wouldn't believe!

Sibi - Try me!

Zoc - We've broken the standard speed of light, we now enter, now get this......Twice the speed of light. It also at this speed that brings us back in time. The group as well as the crew can verify this!

Sibi - I for one find it very hard to swallow,but I saw what I saw!

# Chapter 14

## *Return to ANFORA*

Sibi - That's some story Commander Zoc. I'm surprised you'd try an unproven theory.

Zoc - I really had no choice, once we where pulled into the rift, There was no way to get back to our present location, At our present speed and confirmed by the computer that we couldn't. To break through the rift we needed more speed, a lot more speed. I decided to risk it, and confirmed by the computer. It was go for it or be stranded in another dimension! The computer agreed with me. Thus....We plowed through the rift at twice the speed of light! A very risky business! Sibi - Risky to say the least!

Zoc - I just wish you where there with me.

Sibi - How long was the sustained flight?

Zoc - Less then a minute or so.Once we past through the rift we automatic switched back to standard flight after we where out of the pull of the rifts influence.

Sibi - That means your craft traveled back in time in less than three hours in just under a minute. Zoc - That's right and no ill effects,so far!

Sibi - Do you realize how far we could travel back in time at that speed.

Zoc - Who knows?

Sibi - Once we're back home what's your plans?

Zoc - Plan a trip back in time!

Sibi - That's if the commission will let you, And if they say go for it, then I want to be aboard your first official flight.

Zoc - I wouldn't have it any other way my friend.

Sibi - To tell the truth I'd go on that trip even if the commission turned you down!

Zoc - I'm sure the commission will make the right decision. But I'm with you on this one Sibi. Sibi - I know the space commission as well as you and don't think for one minute that they'll go along with this!

Zoc - I have my doubts too!

Sibi - First they'd say theres not any good reason to go back in time, And if you did go back, change one little thing etc etc......

Zoc - I hear you, they would also say changes made by us could cause complication beyond belief, therefore would decline such a trip! I know them only to well myself!

Sibi - We both have the commission down pat!

Zoc - But if they did turn me down I'd go anyway.

Sibi - Who's to know! Nothing ventured nothing gained!

Zoc - Well Sibi,For now it's back to ANFORA, I'll see you to the transport.

Sibi - Good bye Zoc.

Zoc - Good bye for now, See me after we land.

The group heads for the bridge to see Zoc. Tom - Hi Zoc!

Zoc - Hello Tom, John, Girls!

Tom - We did hit twice the speed of light! Yes?

Zoc - We certainly did, My friend,We did!

Tom - Such a smooth change over, Hardly felt a thing,I just saw a blur at the porthole.

Zoc - I was as surprised as you where, an unproven theory that worked for us.

Heidi - My heart was in my throat, I was sure the ship would fall apart!

Zoc - I gambled with all our lives,It could have gone either way. But Luck was on our side and we won! But I'm certain we would have died if the chance was not taken. One thing I did count on was the computer and the integrity of this ship. I wasn't to sure about us.

Connie - At least it's all behind us.

Tom - What happens to us when we get to ANFORA?

Zoc - Nothing. You go on your merry way, You all have plenty of money to go wherever you care or wish to go.

Heidi - But we were sent to the new planet for stealing your craft.

Zoc - It's not your fault that the planet had to be evacuated, They wouldn't leave you there to die now would they?

Tom - Your always so certain of everything.

Zoc - All the time we've been together you still forget the time difference!

Those who judged you are either to old or dead by now to care one way or the other. It took you twentyfive light years going and returning, plus the one and a half years on the planet.

John - Since we age ever so slowly in space we tend to forget time all together.

Zoc - Now you've got it. since I first met all four of you / You where just in your early twenties, Yes, well you've aged a little over four years thats all, no more no less.

John - that's amazing, we've traveled over two hundred fifty light years and we're still in our prime!

Connie - What about this new speed, How do we age then?

Zoc - Well we did go back in time, But it's any-bodys guess at this time untill we can do an extensive test then and only then can we evaluate the findings.

Tom - I would venture that we would get younger.

Zoc - Wishful thinking, but let's not grasp at straws, shall we people.

Zoc - Of course anythings possible, Like I said only a full test could prove this oneway or the other. It is an interesting hypothesis.

John - Can your next flight out be at this new speed?

Zoc - I was resently speaking to Sibi about such a flight. We agreed that knowing the space commission they'd probably turn us down.

John - What if they gave the okay, Would you take us on your next trip?

Zoc - I assume you speak for the whole group? The group yes we all want to go!

Zoc - Then I'll hold you to that agreement! Well so far I have a crew and a first mate, That makes a total of six, Of course there will be many more who would jump at the chance.

Connie - You mean Sibi as first mate right?

Zoc - That's right and when we get to ANFORA I'll ask Tolo too.

Zoc - Well then just sit back and enjoy the flight back to ANFORA! months pass

ANFORA was not far off now and in a few more weeks and they would be landing back where they had left twenty six and a half years ago, How much change had been made since they where there? During this time all the group could think of was the new found speed, They all entisapated in though of Zoc's next flight, would there be one ? They all prayed that the commission would grant Zocs dream and theirs.

It wouldn't be long before the'd be landing and Zoc would go to the commision and ask their permission for a test flight! They wondered how long would it take to get a answer........

ANFORA in sight

They'd be landing soon now and hopes where high. Now all they had to do is wait for the outcome and Zoc!

Soon after landing the group where taken to Zocs apartment complex.

Zoc talked to Tolo and told him of his plans and said Sibi and the group would be joining him on this quest and he would like him to be part of this adventure?

Tolo didn't hesitate, He would join with the others.

Zoc went straight to the commission with the news breaking twice the speed of light. It was not a theory anymore, But a proven fact, It could be done and he did it.

The crew that was aboard Zocs craft had told every one of their flight of twice the speed of light. This the commission already knew. News travels fast on ANFORA, BUT NOT that fast! the crew had beaten him to the punch. He was looking forward to telling the commission first!, Alas it still didn't kill his enthusism one bit! Right off the bat Zoc asked the commission for a prolonged test flight.

The commission stated that they'd think about it and get back to him with their findings on Zocs proposal.

Zoc was also told that in the event that such a flight where granted, He'd have to have a complete crew of volunteers or it would be a no go!

Zoc arrives at the apartment to tell them he just came back from the commission.

John - Do you have any idea how soon you'll receive word?

Zoc - I have not way of knowing, some times they respond quick and at other times it takes weeks or even months! No way can you predict which way the wind will shift.

Tom - I'm hoping for a quick response!

John - We spend so much waiting in our lives, I believe we spend one third of it waiting for something or another!

Heidi - Well heres another third coming up!

Zoc - I'm apprehensive myself, Just hang in there.

Connie - Let's forget all this for now and go out and enjoy ourselves for a change.

Heidi - Very good idea! Let's do the town gang! You to Zoc!

Zoc - I'm game.

John - We'll tour the city and then stop and then go to some fine restaurant, I'm sure Zoc knows plenty of good ones!

Two months pass

Finally Zoc was summoned to the space center. With fingers crossed he enters the room. Head commissiner, Good afternoon Commander Zoc. Please be seated.

Zoc - Good afternoon Sir.

Well Commander Zoc we've given full consideration to this this test flight,and have come to the conclusion that going back in time serves no meaningful purpose, Therefore we must decline your request......maybe at a future date we may reconsider. Until then it has been denied. I'm very sorry Commander Zoc. Good day.

Good day says Zoc.

Zoc is heart sick. He thinks to himself Sibi was right and deep down I knew the answer too Why did I convince myself they'd okay a flight! I should have known better.

Back at the apartment the group heard from Zoc that he was summoned to the space center, They waited to find out the results, All hoping for good news.

Zoc was now heading back to tell the group the Commissins decision.

Zoc stops off to telephone both Sibi and Tolo to tell them of the commissions findings. Meet me at my apartment at four thirty, I just don't want to tell the group the bad news by myself,understood.

Both agreed and would meet him at the apartment.

Zoc - Right on time, shall we go up and relate the news!

Sibi - Yes the sooner the better.

A knock at the door brought an instant reply.

John - Hello Zoc I wasn't expecting Sibi and Tolo come in.

Zoc Hello gang.

What's the verdict gentlemen ?

Zoc - I'm afraid I have bad news!

Tom - They turned you down?

Zoc - They said that a flight of such a nature would serve no meaningful purpose!

Heidi - Oh Zoc! I'm so sorry.

Zoc They said they where sorry too.

John - They turned down an opportunity of a life time. Are they nuts!!!!

Connie - Take it to a higher authority.

Zoc - There is no higher authority, Thats that.

Tom - So what do we do give them the last word?

Zoc - We have no choice!

Tom - But we do! When your assigned to your next flight, do what you want to do!

Zoc - I don't beleive what I'm hearing, are you suggesting I go against the Commissioners orders?

John - Come now Zoc you where planning that all along. Who do you think your fooling!

Heidi - I think we know you a lot better then you know yourself, admit it.

Zoc - you know these humans are going to get us in hot water..

Sibi - They don't need your help for that!

Zoc - Does everybody know what i'm going to do!

John - We know that your heart is in this or
should I say was in testing twice the speed of
light, But whatever the commission or anybody else
says you still want that flight. Thats obvious to all of use!

Tolo - They know you like a book an open book at that.

Zoc - Yes your right about all of it. I had a dream but we can't have everything in life!

Who am I trying to fool, You see right through me like a pane of glass. The next flight out we're going to keep our destiny and go where no one has gone -I pledge this to you.

Zoc, Sibi and Tolo leave the apartment and head back to the Space Center.

Sibi - Iv'e heard you have a flight plan coming up Zoc.

Zoc - Yes. In two weeks, Why?

Sibi - There was nothing posted on the bulletin board.

Zoc - Just another flight, so what. Tolo - you said Sibi and I would be on your next flight out.

Zoc - That's right if I where going to twice the speed of light, which I'm not.

Sibi - All three of us can go on this flight with you.

Zoc - Why would you and Tolo both give up your command to go with me?

Sibi - To where we were goingwith you before, if the Commission hadn't fouled up your plans, so why not.

Zoc - Tolo! does Sibi talk for you too?

Tolo - No sibi doesn't speak for me, I've already stated I'd go on your next flight.

Sibi - I listened to John this afternoon, he reminds me of you, bold and brave, willing to take chances.

Zoc - Tolo are you and Sibi suggesting I do what John said?

Why not! says Tolo.

Zoc - Tolo!

Zoc - Between you two and John we'll all be shot if caught.

Sibi - I agree with Tolo, why not! You must be getting old Commander, my old friend, You never worried before

Zoc - Sighs, Should we?

Both, Yes.

Zoc - Okay, It's our necks if we're caught!

Sibi - That's our old Commander.

Zoc - I'll need John, he's the master mind of such things!

Tolo - what about the others?

Zoc - I don't think the others have changed their minds about going. Generally speaking they follow each other, where one goes they all go!

Sibi - Then lets get going. We need a crew we can trust and count on.

Zoc - I don't think either one of you will have a problem finding a crew, I myself have several people in mind.

Sibi - I know many of my old crew can be trusted.

Zoc - And you Tolo!

Tolo - Same here.

Zoc - I'll get in touch with the group and tell them, In the mean time you both have your job s to do, Get a crew, we have only two weeks left!

At the apartment

Zoc knocks at the door and is greeted by John.

Zoc - we though of what you said John, And we're to go for it! Two weeks will be our lift off date!

Yahoo! Great news!

Zoc - The others are out looking for a crew at this minute.

Tom - So your actually going through with Johns idea!

Zoc - Absolutely!

Tom - two weeks isn't much time to find a trusting crew!

Zoc - Trust me Sibi and Tolo, we'll get the best of the best for this voyage, count on it! Plus we won't need as many crew personel, a small crew will be sufficient and a medium size craft will suit our needs just fine.

Connie - Where are we going back to?

Zoc - First things first Connie, we need a trusted crew, then hand pick the ones we want.

Tom - But how many can you trust?

Zoc - I'm not going to tell this new crew anything about our twice the speed of light plan, it's just to risky. There are many who would give their lives for us, still only after we pick the ones who will be going with us will be told of our secret mission.

Tom - Will the commission allow us to go on this trip?

Zoc - probably they will, They'd be only to glad to get rid of you four, for a while anyway!

John - Out of sight out of mind.

Zoc - You've got it John.

They all laugh.

Zoc - Some of the crew I chose are real close to me and I have no doubt that they will accompany us. You know most of them, But I'm not saying who they maybe at this time.

Tom - Why can't you tell us who these people are?

Zoc - Because some may already have plans of their own.

Zoc - I'll be going now. Have to check on something.

The papers had pictures of Zoc standing in front of the craft that made history. Under the picture was the story of how Commander Zoc conquered Twice the speed of light. He was an instant celebrity. Zoc didn't like the limelight, he just wanted to be left alone. But he did make use of his new found fame. Recruitng many new faces. He told all that inquired that in time he would consider each and everyone, he would contact them when he had made up his mind.

Tolo and Sibi had also taken in quite a number of men and women.

Now came the time to pick the best and weed out the rest, those that where chosen signed a pledge and loyalty to Command Zoc and His Officers. All was working out, Sibi and Tolo where pleased.

Zoc's next plan was to get to the apartment before dark.

On arrival Zoc knocks at the door. Tom answers it.

Come in Zoc, we're ready when you are.

Zoc - Get the rest of the group I want to say some thing.

Tom - Sure thing, be right back, moments later

Tom - Well here we be!

Tom - Now that we're here Zoc, What's on your mind?.

Zoc - We've discussed this before many times, we're in serious trouble if we're caught!

John - We know all that! Please hear us out,before you say another word. Tom and I discused the very problem you face and come up with this...now listen closely, we travel back in time, do our thing, then go back in time again to the time we first left! Can you see what we're driving at?

Zoc - Yes! The present, we go back, then we go back to the present which is now the past!

Great, Why didn't I think of that before!You two are the best thing that has happened to me in a long time, a very long time. To think we had problems where there was none!

John - then we go?

Zoc - I was always ready to go, I just had some doubts, I'm fine now!

John - You have chosen the crew?

Zoc - Everything is all set to go, crew included.

Well Gentlemen and ladies you may board the craft now. Everyone else is aboard.

Heidi - How long before take off.?

Zoc - exactly twenty minutes from now so go to your cabins, Sibi will show you the way,by the time your settled in your cabin it'll be close to take off time.

John - Heres Luck to all of us. See you later Zoc.

Lead the way Sibi.

Babe - Commander Zoc we have clearence from the tower.

Zoc - Babe take her up!

Babe - Yes commander Zoc.

intercom buckle up

The craft rises slowly,then gains speed as she enters above ANFORAS atmosphere, Once in deep space she goes to the standard speed.

Zoc - Summons the group to the bridge.

Zoc - Tom, John you two are asigned to the computer. Good news we have " BABE " with us again.

John - That's very good news.

Zoc - Connie you and Heidi will be working with Ada again.

Heidi - Ada,Wonderful!

Connie - May we leave the bridge and go find Ada?

Zoc - I see we may have a problem here if we just go wondering off. I think Tolo should give you a full tour,then you'll all know where everything is Tomorrow is soon enough for you to go to work!

The group retired for the night. When morning came they dressed and headed straight for the bridge.

Good morning Zoc came the cry from the group!

Zoc - Ah, good morning, Have you had breakfast yet ?

Not yet came the reply, We where anxious to get started!

Zoc - Well we can't have that, lets eat.

Zocs instructions where to scan a new group of stars and seek out intelligent life, but Zoc and the others had their own plans! calling the group together after breakfast to discuss their destination. Now that we're together let's decide our next adventure!

Connie - What about Sibi and Tolo, shouldn't they be here?

Zoc - I asked them both, they will go wherever we go. So let's proceed.

Heidi - I have a suggestion, Zoc you remember Lucy Burrows.?

Zoc - Of course! Pauls wife.

Heidi - Lacy died so young. If we could go back to that day when Sibi beamed us aboard.Well there must be some way to get medical care that may save her life!

Zoc - Sounds good, except Paul probably had Lucy see a Doctor back home! what can we do that your Doctors back home couldn't?

Connie - Paul knew nothing of her condition, Lucy never told him, and yes, Lucy did see a Doctor,the operation would cost well over thirty thousand Dollars, so she decided not to tell Paul. I knew Lucy had a bad heart back in high school and swore me to secrecy. I've never told anyone this until now!

Zoc - Then let's proceed to earth. We can come up with a plan on the way.

Babe set a couse for earth at twice the speed of light,Our arrival time should be set for June twenty second nineteen hundred seventy three.

Babe - Yes Commander Zoc

Zoc - Babe after you make your calculations give us time to secure before engaging.

Babe - Understood Commander Zoc.

two minutes lapsed

Babe - calculations done, engaging in three minutes.

intercom buckle up

Zoc - Thanks Babe it's in your ball park now!

Babe - Ball park? That doesn't compute Commander Zoc!

That means we're in your hands!

Babe - Now I understand commander Zoc.

That night

Zoc I think I have come up with a solution. I will write myself a letter to myself and give it to Sibi to give to himself, inturn the first Sibi will beam up with the first group and later he will find the letter and bring it to the first Zoc.

John - Good plan, lets hope that Sibi can plant a letter on himself without knowing!

Sibi - I know the exact place where I can stow away the letter.

Zoc - This all depends on you Sibi, please don't be seen by anyone.

Sibi - You can count on me Zoc!

Heidi - I'm so excited, It's like a mystery . unfolding before us.

Tom - The plan seems flawless, just one thing Zoc what do you plan on writing in this letter? Zoc I have some idea,but it needs work if I can convince my other self that the letter is not a joke!

# Chapter 15

## *Dajavu*

Babe - Were over earth commander Zoc!

Zoc - Thank you Babe.

Zoc - Okay John, I think this plan of ours will work just fine.

June 21, 1973

Tom - Looks like a great place. Let's find a hotel. All agree. Not far down the road Connie says, Over there. Tom pulls in and parks. Well Gang! Here at last. Let's register. They all pile out, grabbing their luggage and enter the hotel. Tom rings bell.

Desk Clerk - May I be of assistance? We'd like a room please.

Clerk - How many in your party?

Tom - My wife and I.

Clerk - How long will you be staying?

Tom - Umm...He turns to John. John shrugs his shoulder... holding up three fingers.

Tom - Okay, three days then.

Clerk - Cash or credit card?

Tom - Credit card.

Clerk - Runs credit card through machine. Please register.

Turns book around. Tom signs Mr. and Mrs. Thomas Mon'e

Pennsylvania.

Clerk - First, fifth floor or sixth.

Tom - Fifth, I could use the exercise.

Clerk - We do have an elevator.

Tom - So much for exercise...

Clerk - Your key, sir. Room 512. Boy - bags.

John - Three days for us too. Same floor please.

Clerk - I only have 2 on the sixth, 1 on the first floor.

John - Okay, we'll take the one on the first floor.

Clerk - Cash/credit?

John - Credit card. (Machine run)

Clerk - Please sign the register.

Mr. and Mrs. John Hodges, Pennsylvania.

Clerk - Your room key 12..boy, bags.

Tom - I should have asked that we be on the same floor.

Clerk - I can change it!

John - NO, that's okay. Let it stay as is.

Clerk - We have a fine western dinner in back of the hotel (points). Show your room key to your waiter and receive a 10% discount.

John - Great...you hear that Tom?

Got it - see you around six in the lobby for dinner.

John - Sounds good. We'll be ready. We have over two hours till then.

That evening they all meet and wander over to the dinner.

Heidi - Dinner! It's gigantic - it's more like a New York City restaurant.

Connie to Heidi - That was an understatement. It's awesome.

Tom - Well, let's go in. On entering they all stared around the spacious hall. High timbered ceiling, from the rafters hung large wagon wheels to light the hall. An old-fashioned bar with spitoon and all. On the walls were plowshares, pitchforks, yolks, pictures and murals depicating the by-gone years.

Maitre'de - How many in your party? Four came the reply.

Maitre'de snaps finger...hostess comes over. follow me please. Everyone is still looking around as the hostess escorted them to a table.

Hostess - How's this? All agree. Fine, thank you.

Hostess - I'll send back a waitress to help you. Shortly a waitress approaches their table. Waitress - Good evening, everyone. My name is Gail and I'll be your waitress for this evening.

Everyone smiles and says Hi.

Waitress - Your menu and wine/liquor list. Would you care for a drink before dinner?

Tom - Ladies first.

Connie - I'll have a white wine.

Heidi - A Shirley Temple please.

Waitress - Very good. Gentlemen?

Tom - Large beer, Sam Adams.

John - Sounds good, make that two.

Waitress - I'll be back soon with your drinks. (Leaves)

After some small chit-chat the waitress brings the drinks white wine for you, Shirley Temple for you and two beers.

Enjoy your drinks. Just raise your hands if you need me.

Soup and salad bar is to your left.

Heidi - You know Connie, I have the strange feeling we've done this all before!

Connie - It does, doesn't it!

Aboard space craft

Zoc - One more day to go then we'll see how this plan works out.

Heidi - Did you finish your letter?

Zoc - Completed and ready to go now everyone get a little shut eye. Good night gang!

Back on earth

The following morning six of them strike out for the stables.

Red (ranch-hand) had seleced the horses. Each party had a canteen and some sandwiches and off they went.

Aboard Zocs craft So far so good! everything as before.

(Back on Earth) We're just a short distance now. Replies Tom.

John - Hey Mr. Horse is limping. Hold on. John dismounts, checks. He had a stone in his shoe. You go on ahead.

I'll catch up with you.

Back aboard Zoc's craft. Okay Sibi get ready to beam down.

You have the note! Asks Zoc.

Sibi - Yes Zoc.

Sibi beams down and waits out of sight.

Paul - You know I have the strangest feeling we've done this before.

Connie - Same here, I've had it since yesterday at the Dinner table. What about you Tom?

It certainly appears that way.

Connie - Whatever you do Heidi, Don't scream.

Heidi - Why would I scream?

Connie - If I'm right you'll see!

Sibi - sneaks up to see himself and quietly puts the envelope in his back pack. Then Sibi beams backup.

Zoc - Sibi your other self didn't spot you?

Sibi - I'm so good I fooled myself.

Zoc - Now lets see what else happens!

Aboard the original craft the five are escorted to the decontamination center and John is taken to the hospital, mean time Sibi finds the envelope address to Commander Zoc.

Sibi - I found this letter in my backpack Commander Zoc it's addressed to you. Zoc takes the envelope written in his own hand.To Commander Zoc. For your eyes only! Zoc opens the envelpoe, pulls out the letter and before he reads the contents, he dismisses Sibi. Zoc, It starts..so you don't think this is a trick I'll call you by your nickname your Uncle Cabo called you when you where a child.No one else including your Aunt Beda, or anyone else called you "Benturwekz." Big man in little pants, you hated that name,also this little token you've carried all your life. A small coin with your name and birthday on one side and on the other, The family crest. Best of everything Dad. Zoc reaches into his pocket and takes out the coin, identical right down to the scratches. You Zoc have exceeded time travel! aboard your craft theres a man called Professor Paul Burrows and his wife.

She has a very serious heart condition and if not given proper care, she will die on Anfora at the age of thirty four, if I remember correctly. Lucy has never told Paul of her condition. I know I can depend on you. I will not tell you about the others but trust your instinct.

They are all good people. Your computer will confirm my location. Ten miles due east of your position. At exactly six o'clock send a signal over to my craft to be sure you understand. I will acknowledge back on the same frequency one minute later.

Zoc there's the signal get ready "Babe" on my count!
Now send!
Babe - Signal sent ... a message follows Commander Zoc.
What's it say Babe? says Zoc.
Good luck,. self...
Zoc - Laughs, I'm funny.
Babe - Whats funny Commander Zoc?
Personal Babe, nothing at all.
That night Zoc speaks to the others.
Zoc - Everything went off without a hitch. I'm glad or I should I say very pleased at the outcome.
Heidi - Wow Lucy is going to love a normal life.

Zoc - Paul is going to wonder how I knew his wife had a serious heart condition!

John - Let him wonder, as long as he can have Lucy for many years to come.

Tom - Sure Zoc, you can't be wondering what he is wondering.

Connie - We should thank Sibi for getting that envelope on to himself without noticing.

John - This conversation is getting weird.

Sibi - Sneaking up on yourself, reading a letter you wrote to yourself and not knowing its contents is more then weird.

Zoc - So far the only ones who know what We've done, is us! The rest of the crew only knows that we returned to earth in the past, but no explanation was ever given.

Tolo - Shall I inform them?

Zoc - Yes Tolo use the intercom.

John - I was just thinking how do we know for sure everything turned out as planned?

Zoc - You mean conformation?

John - Watch!

Zoc - That's a problem only "Babe" can figure out. Don't forget we went back in time, to retrace our steps to the time , well after your escaped from ANFORA

John - Well thats in the past. There is no reason why we can't go back again and check on Lucy. No!

Zoc - That makes sense. Lets go . Babe, we want to head back to Anfora, time frame just after John took the space craft from Anfora to earth.

Babe - It can be done Commander Zoc

Zoc - Then head us back "Babe"

Babe - Yes Commander Zoc.

Zoc - We are taking a big chance on being picked up by other craft in the area.

John - We can out run them.

Zoc - Only deeper into the past •

John - Solution, have "Babe" contact the other "Babe" and have the message that was recieved from the commission on burrows.

Zoc - Thats very good then we don't have to go anywhere near Anforia! John you amaze me.

John - Ah shucks twerent notten

Zoc - Babe

Babe - Yes Commander Zoc

Zoc - In your memory bank, look up the date and time we recieved the second message from the borrows estate.

Babe - Yes Commander Zoc.

Babe - Message reads: To Commander Zoc from space center Anfora, Professor Burrows retained his position in the Anfora chemical plant. Two years later he came up with a chemical process which made him famous and wealthy.

Promoted to head chemist, Professor Paul Burrows died a the age of seventy-six and was survived by his wife of forty two yeasrs. She died in her sleep one year later, she was seventy-two.

Headquarters, ANFORA Space Center.

Signed Ludi Meterozo.

Zoc - Now that's all over, Your otherselves have left for ANFORA,Lucys okay and now it's time for you four to decide what you want to do!

Sibi - Why not stay here on earth and finish your vacation? You could even raise a family!

Tom - Just one little problem, earth will not be here in the future, what happens to our heirs!?

John - Also, we can't go back to ANFORA!

Connie - We can't stay here, so what do we do?

Zoc - Maybe the Commission was right after all, it serves no useful purpose.

John - Maybe Sibis right,we could stay here on earth, raise a family then in ten or twenty years Zoc can pick us up.

Zoc - I don't think so!

John - Why not?

Zoc - I think "BABE" could answer that one.

Babe.

Yes commander Zoc.

Zoc - Babe is it possible to bring the group back to ANFORA, say in twenty years from now?

Babe - It is possible if we travel at the standard speed and land. But theres a hitch.

(one) how could you account for there age difference between you and the crew,

(two) how do you account for the missing time,

(third) your craft was supposed to be looking for intelligent life two hundred light years away. You'd arrive back way ahead of schedule.

Zoc - Well thats that!

John - If nothing else, we did accomplish one thing, and that was to save Lucy!

Tom - There's still a solution, get this, If we go back in time again to where Zocs craft

is suppose to be......we continue from there.

Zoc - Yes we could, but there still would be two of us. There doesn't seem to be a solution to our dilemma!

Zoc - Babe!

Babe - Yes Commander Zoc.

Zoc - The reasons you gave us are not feasible, do you have any alternatives?

Babe - I see only two.

(one) Go back to your original assigment with the group and the quest to find intelligent life.

(two) The only other solution is stay in the past forever. Never to approach yourselves, the best of the two. Remember the past is the past, and the future is the future, for at this time we know little of what will happen since we did alter the past. Commander Zoc.

Zoc - Thank you Babe.

Zoc - Right at this moment the dilemma we face seems to have no perfect out come,we're at a deadend no matter what we try to conjure up!

John - Babe returning to Zocs assignment means a total of four hundred light years in space,there must be something else?

Babe - Once you go back in time , you can never catch up with the present until it's the past John.

Zoc - Babe why didn't you say so before?

Babe - You never asked,Commander Zoc.

Zoc - Well crew it looks like we're stuck here in the past.

Sibi - Well thats life. We may as well see the or explore the galaxy.

Zoc - I guess your right Sibi,I'll have to inform the crew of this turn of events!

Tom - That could mean trouble!

Zoc - I have no choice but to be honest with them! For now let's all get some rest,tomorrow we'll figure what we'll do.

The group head back to their quartes.

John - Zoc's right theres not a damn thing we can do about it.

Tom - It's to bad we can't go forward at twice the speed of light, then our problems would be over.

John - Your right as rain my friend!

Heidi - John, John wake up.

John - Whats the matter honey?

Heidi - You've been twitching and turning all night and mumbling something in your sleep.

John - Yeah! Just a weird dream thats all.

Heidi - It must have been some dream!

John - What time is it?

Heidi - six o'clock, now tell me about your dream?

John - I'll tell you during breakfast,we don't have much time.

After breakfast

John - Well thats all of it, what do you think?

Heidi - Thats some dream alright!

John - Hey! What time is it?

Heidi - Six-forty five.

John - We'd better hurry,I hate being late and we still have to pick up Connie and Tom.

Heidi - Vacation time here we come.

John - But this time we're heading south not WEST!!!!!

## THE END

Heidi - Whats this small tuning fork for??????

# About the Author

Born on January 1936 in Flushing, Long Island, New York. I was raised and educated in White Plains, New york. Moved to Connecticut in 1958. I took a course on television repair, obtained my state license four years later. I stayed in this field for most of my adult life. I've been married twice and have five children,and twelve grandchildren. After many years of retirement, I decided to write a book.